THE FUGITIVE
FROM CORINTH

Caroline Lawrence

The Roman Mysteries: Book X

THE FUGITIVE
FROM CORINTH

ROARING BROOK PRESS
New Milford, Connecticut

Copyright © 2005 Roman Mysteries Ltd.
Published by Roaring Brook Press
Roaring Brook Press is a division of Holtzbrinck Publishing Holdings
Limited Partnership
143 West Street, New Milford, Connecticut 06776.
First Published in the United Kingdom in 2005 by Orion Children's Books, London
Maps by Richard Russell Lawrence copyright © 2005 by Orion Children's Books.

Library of Congress Cataloging-in-Publication Data
Lawrence, Caroline.
The fugitive from Corinth / Caroline Lawrence.—1st American ed.
p. cm.—(The Roman mysteries ; bk. 10)
Summary: Flavia and her friends pursue tutor Aristo from Corinth to Athens when he
escapes after being accused of committing a brutal attack on Flavia's father.

ISBN-13: 978-1-59643-083-9 (alk. paper)
ISBN-10: 1-59643-083-4 (alk. paper)

[1. Mistaken identity-Fiction. 2. Brothers-Fiction. 3. Rome-History-Empire,
30 B.C.–476 A.D.-Fiction. 4. Mystery and detective stories.] I. Title. II. Series:
Lawrence, Caroline. Roman mysteries ; bk. 10.
PZ7.L425Fug 2006
[Fic]-dc22
2006000048

Roaring Brook Press books are available for special promotions and premiums.
For details, contact: Director of Special Markets, Holtzbrinck Publishers

First American Edition October 2006

Printed in the United States of America

2 4 6 8 10 9 7 5 3 1

To my wonderful brother Dan

quem numquam mihi in

mentem necare venit

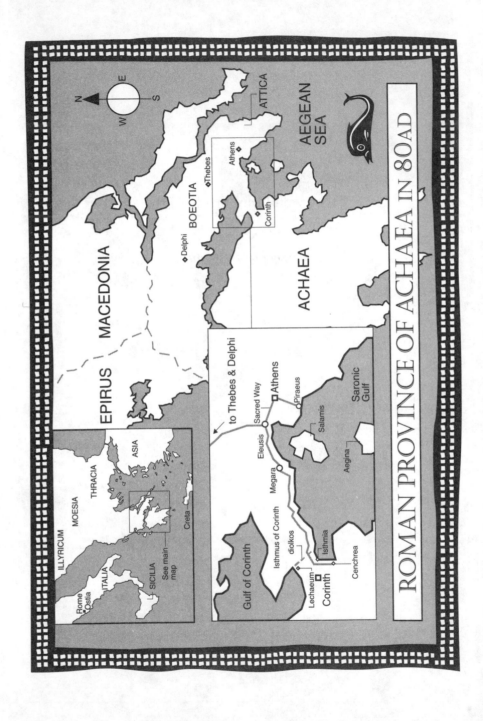

ROMAN PROVINCE OF ACHAEA IN 80AD

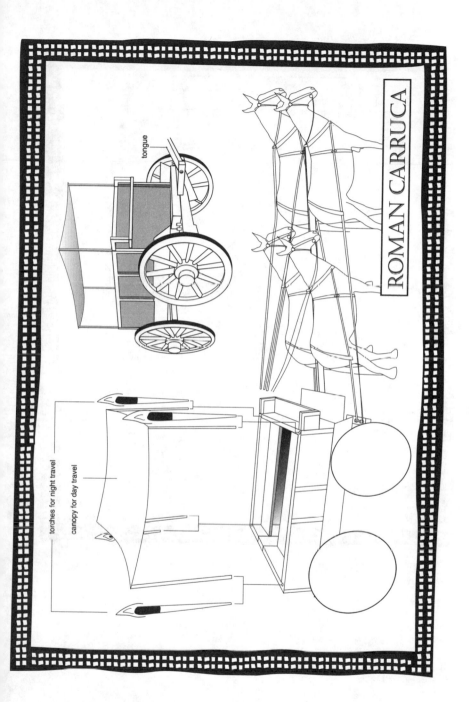

ROMAN CARRUCA

tongue

torches for night travel

canopy for day travel

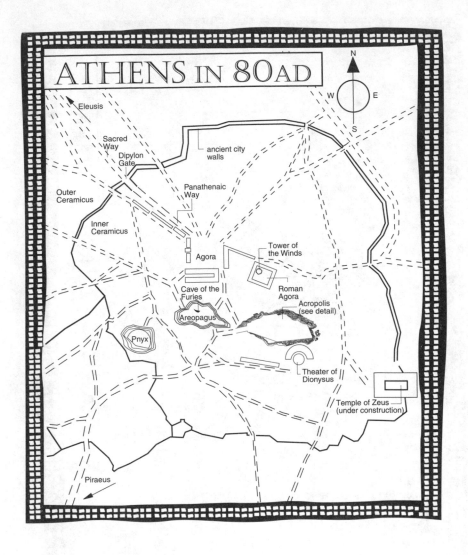

ATHENS IN 80AD

N
W E
S

Eleusis

Sacred Way

Dipylon Gate

ancient city walls

Outer Ceramicus

Panathenaic Way

Inner Ceramicus

Agora

Tower of the Winds

Cave of the Furies

Roman Agora

Areopagus

Acropolis (see detail)

Pnyx

Theater of Dionysus

Temple of Zeus (under construction)

Piraeus

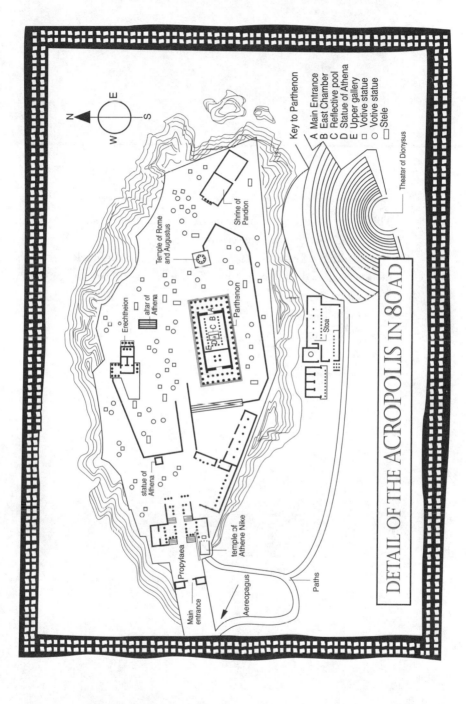

DETAIL OF THE ACROPOLIS IN 80 AD

N
W — E
S

Key to Parthenon
A Main Entrance
B East Chamber
C Reflective pool
D Statue of Athena
E Upper gallery
□ Votive statue
○ Votive statue
▭ Stele

Theater of Dionysus

Shrine of Pandion

Temple of Rome and Augustus

Erechtheion

altar of Athena

Parthenon

statue of Athena

Stoa

Propylaea

temple of Athene Nike

Main entrance

Aereopagus

Paths

This story takes place in Ancient Roman times, so a few of the words may look strange.

If you don't know them, "Aristo's Scroll" at the back of the book will tell you what they mean and how to pronounce them.

Maps at the front will show you the parts of Greece where this story takes place. There is also a drawing of a *carruca,* a Roman carriage.

SCROLL I

"I first met him in Corinth," said the Roman sea captain, Marcus Flavius Geminus, "when he saved my life."

"He saved your life?" A dark-skinned African girl in a yellow tunic sat up straight on her banqueting couch. It was a warm evening in early May. Nubia, the ex-slave girl, and her three friends were dining with the captain in the garden triclinium of Helen's Hospitium, a luxury hotel near Cenchrea, the eastern port of Corinth. Although Marcus Flavius Geminus did not usually allow the children in his household to recline at dinner, this was a special occasion. It was their last day in Greece after their recent adventures in the Greek islands. They were to sail home to Ostia in the morning.

Captain Geminus smiled and nodded. "That's right, Nubia. He saved my life."

"I never knew that, Pater!" The fair-haired girl next to Nubia dipped her hard-boiled egg into a mixture of salt and cumin and took a bite. "Tell us how he saved you." Ten-year-old Flavia Gemina was Nubia's former mistress and Captain Geminus's daughter. She loved stories and mysteries.

Captain Geminus smiled. "When I say Corinth, I mean the port—Lechaeum—rather than the town itself. I was drinking hot sage in a caupona down by the waterfront. I remember it was

1

evening, and raining. I was waiting for the harbormaster. Suddenly four men got up from a nearby table and came over to me."

Flavia's father paused for a moment as a slave girl with dark red hair came through an ivy-covered arch, carrying a light table with various salads on it. She was followed by a big Syrian slave with a candle. The slave girl set the salad table before the central couch while the male slave began to light the garden torches. Nubia could smell vinegar and pine pitch.

"It was only when one of them grabbed my arms and another cut the cord of my money pouch," continued Flavia's father, "that I realized what they were after and started to fight back. But there were four of them and only one of me. They beat me to the ground and then they began to kick me!"

"Oh, Pater!" cried Flavia, putting down her egg. "How terrible!"

He nodded. "I can still remember the taste of sawdust in my mouth. Then I heard what the Greeks call a *paean,* a battle cry. I felt the kicking stop and I looked up to see a young man of about seventeen. He was dripping wet from the rain, and he wielded a broken chair like a club. I've rarely seen anyone so angry. He knocked the leader to the ground and started swinging at the other three." Captain Geminus took a slice of cucumber from his salad. "That's when the other people in the caupona ran to help, but it was his quick action that saved me."

Two dark-haired boys were reclining on a couch opposite the girls. "I've seen him get irritated," said Jonathan, the older of the two, "but I don't think I've ever seen him really angry. Have you, Lupus?"

The younger boy was intent on peeling an egg. Without looking up he grunted yes. Nine-year-old Lupus had no tongue and could not speak.

Flavia grinned. "If you've seen him lose his temper, Lupus, it's probably because you're the one who made him lose it!"

2

Lupus looked up at them and nodded proudly, and they all laughed.

"No, wait!" cried Flavia. "We *have* seen him lose his temper. Remember the stuffed mushrooms last December?"

"Don't remind me," said Jonathan with a groan. "I ate some, too."

Nubia giggled behind her hand.

"What's this?" said Flavia's father with a puzzled smile. "Why would mushrooms make him angry?"

"They were stuffed with a love potion made from gladiator scrapings," said Flavia, trying not to laugh. "You know, the stuff gladiators scrape off after a really good workout: dead skin, oil, sweat, dust . . ."

"He was *so* angry," added Jonathan, "that he said . . . he said . . ." But Jonathan was laughing too hard to finish.

"No, wait!" Flavia held up her hand for silence. "He said—" but then she also dissolved into helpless giggles.

Lupus's shoulders were shaking, too, but he had managed to write something on his wax tablet. Now he held it up:

BY APOLLO I SWEAR I'M GOING TO MURDER HER

At this they all burst out laughing, even Nubia and the captain.

"What's the subject of conversation?"

Everyone turned to see a handsome young man framed in the leafy arched entrance of the garden.

"You!" they all cried, and called out their greetings. Next to the ornamental pool, Jonathan's dog, Tigris, lifted his head from a marrowbone and thumped his tail.

Nubia watched the young man step into the golden torch-light. Had he grown? He seemed taller and more muscular. He wore red leather sandals, and a red woolen cloak over a white tunic. With his smooth tanned skin and curly hair the color

of bronze, she thought her tutor, Aristo, looked just like a
Greek god.

"Did I seem angry that evening?" said Aristo a short time later,
taking a handful of currants from a green glass bowl. "I only remember feeling vexed."

"Then I sincerely hope I never vex you," laughed Flavia's father,
accepting the bowl from Aristo and sprinkling some currants onto
his honey-drizzled yogurt. Both men were barefoot and wearing
short-sleeved white tunics. Although her father was ten years
older than Aristo, it occurred to Flavia that they might almost be
brothers.

"You know, I've always wondered," said her father, "why you
risked your life to help a stranger. For all you know, I might have
been a thief and those four men concerned citizens."

Aristo shrugged. "I'd just had an argument with my brother,"
he said. "I stormed down to the port with the idea of boarding the
first ship out of Corinth. I was so angry that when I came into
the inn and saw those bullies kicking a man on the ground . . . the
next thing I knew I was holding a chair leg and the men were running away."

"Hey!" said Flavia. "That sounds like Hercules after the goddess Juno gave him a potion to drive him mad. When he came
to his senses he saw the dead bodies of his wife and children
lying on the ground and he realized . . ." Her voice trailed off
as she saw the look of reproach in Nubia's golden-brown eyes.
"No," she said quickly. "It's nothing like Hercules. . . ." She
tried to think of a way to change the subject. "Music!" she
cried. "We haven't seen you in weeks, Aristo. Let's play some
music together. Look! I've brought a tambourine! Lupus can
drum on a bowl, and Nubia's wearing her flute around her
neck as usual."

"I'm afraid I don't have my lyre with me."

"Then ask one of the slaves to fetch it from your room. You're in the Orpheus room, aren't you? Nubia and I asked Helen to put you there, in the room next to Pater's. Nubia thought you'd like the room, with the fresco of Orpheus on the wall."

"The landlady showed me the Orpheus room," said Aristo quietly, "and the fresco is very fine. But I don't have my lyre with me tonight."

"But Aristo," said Flavia, "didn't you pack it with the rest of your things?"

"My belongings are all at my parents' house in Corinth."

"But Aristo," said Captain Geminus, pushing himself higher on his elbow, "one of Helen's slaves is going to take us directly to Lechaeum tomorrow at dawn. It will delay us if we have to go into Corinth to get your things."

"I'm sorry, Marcus," said Aristo, "but I'm not going with you tomorrow. I know we had an agreement that I work for you until Flavia reached a marriageable age, but my parents are getting old and infirm—my father's blind, you know—and so I've decided to stay here."

Flavia exchanged a horrified glance with Nubia. "You're not sailing home with us?" she cried.

"No," said Aristo. "I'm staying here in Corinth."

Flavia's father swung his bare feet onto the platform of their dining couch. "I don't understand, Aristo. What are you saying?"

"Is there any way . . . Will you release me from my contract?"

Captain Geminus stared down at the liquid reflection of the torches in the rectangular pool at his feet. "I don't know. This is so sudden." He looked up. "It's not just that Flavia and her friends will be losing a tutor, but you've been my secretary and accountant for three years, and I don't know where I'll find . . . Aristo, is it more money you want? Because we've done very well financially on this trip, and soon I'll be in a position to—" He stopped and looked around at them. The evening breeze was making the

5

torches flutter; in their flickering light it was hard to read the expression on his face.

"Let's discuss this privately, up in my room."

Aristo nodded. The two men bent to lace their sandals, then rose from the couch.

"Aristo!" cried Flavia. "You won't leave without saying goodbye, will you?"

"Of course not." He smiled at them. "I'll spend the night here and go across to the ship with you tomorrow."

He turned and followed Captain Geminus through the ivy arch and out of the flickering circle of torchlight into the darkness of the garden.

"Oh no!" said Flavia, after they'd gone. "What will we do without Aristo? Why won't he come back to Ostia with us?"

"He said something about staying here because of his parents," said Jonathan. "Parents can be a big responsibility."

Suddenly Lupus hissed and put his finger to his lips. At the same moment Tigris lifted his head from his bone and growled.

They all stopped to listen, but apart from the sound of the breeze in the treetops and the tinkle of windchimes in the courtyard, there was no sound.

"What is it, Tigris?" asked Nubia.

"What is it, Lupus?" asked Jonathan.

Lupus pointed behind Flavia. She and Nubia both twisted on their couch, but all they could see behind them was a circle of leaves glowing bright green in the light of the flickering torch.

Tigris growled again.

"What?" Flavia turned back to Lupus to find him scribbling on his wax tablet. When he held it up a moment later, she gasped.

SOMETHING IN THE BUSHES BEHIND YOU, Lupus had written. SOMETHING BIG!

SCROLL II

Thinking quickly, Lupus grasped a handful of currants from the green glass bowl and hurled them at the shrubs behind Flavia.

Instantly, something exploded from the leaves with a staccato warning cry. Lupus yelled, Tigris barked, and Flavia leaped off her dining couch.

A blackbird flew up into the dark blue sky.

Lupus watched the bird disappear and then looked down at Flavia, who stood up to her knees in the ornamental pool. She slowly raised her head and glared at Lupus.

"It was only a blackbird," she growled.

Lupus felt a grin spread across his face and he gave her an exaggerated shrug of apology.

But Tigris was on all four feet now, barking steadily at the bushes.

"What is it, boy?" Jonathan slipped off the couch and circled around to the rhododendron bushes behind the girls' couch. Tigris followed, wagging his tail. "Do you smell something else hiding in there?" Jonathan parted the leaves of the bushes. "Something apart from that terrifying bird?" He disappeared among the shrubs.

"Be careful, Jonathan!" Flavia stepped out of the pool and bent to wring the water from the sodden hem of her best blue tunic.

For a moment there was no sound but the wind. Then:

"Dear gods, it's horrible . . ." came Jonathan's muffled voice from the bushes, and they all looked up.

"It's Medusa!" he yelled and pushed his contorted face out from between two branches. He had stuck out his tongue and ruffled his curly hair and flipped his eyelids back to give himself a terrible staring grin. "Blahhhh!" he cried.

Flavia and Nubia both screamed, and Lupus burst out laughing; this time both girls stood knee-deep in the ornamental pool.

"Flavia, are you awake?"

Flavia sighed and rolled over in her bed to face Nubia in hers. Both their beds were as high as dining couches, and as narrow, but they were comfortable. A tiny oil lamp filled the room with a soft apricot glow. Outside, the evening breeze had become a blustery wind that was rattling shutters, slamming doors, and exciting the wind chimes.

"Who can sleep with all that noise?" said Flavia with a sigh.

"I will miss Aristo. Will you?"

"Of course. I'll miss him terribly. I can't imagine who'll teach us now."

"Aristo is a not a freedman, is he?"

"No. He was never a slave." Flavia yawned. "He's a free man rather than a freedman."

"Flavia, what is contract?"

"It's a written agreement between two people. Are you thinking of Aristo's contract with Pater?"

"Yes."

"I think Aristo agreed to be my tutor for five years, and Pater promised to pay him a certain amount and also to allow him to visit his parents for a few weeks each year. He's served us for three years, so according to the contract he should stay at least two more."

"What if persons disagree the contract?"

"If either of the two people breaks the contract, then one of them has to give the other some money. I think it's called compensation."

"What if Aristo does not have money to pay your father?" asked Nubia.

"I don't know," murmured Flavia, rolling onto her back. "But Aristo is very clever. He'll think of something. . . ."

Nubia was silent after that, and Flavia must have drifted off, for she had no idea how much time had passed when a loud bang woke her. The noise came again. One of the bronze shutters outside their window had come free of its latch and was striking the wall. Flavia slid down from her bed and went to the window. She opened the latticework screen and leaned out. The warm wind whipped her hair and brought the smell of the sea. As she began to fasten the shutter to its outside wall, she thought she heard a man's cry from somewhere within the hospitium.

She pulled her head back into the room and listened. Next door Tigris had begun to bark. She heard the cry come again.

"Pater?" whispered Flavia.

"What's happening?" asked Nubia, pushing back her covers.

"I'm not sure." Flavia took the bronze night-light from its table and moved to the door. "That sounded like Pater. . . ."

Her heart was thumping as she pulled back the heavy curtain of their doorway and went out into the dark corridor with Nubia close behind her. The wall torches had been burning when they had gone to bed, but a slave must have put them out. It was black as pitch out there with only a small globe of light from her oil lamp.

As Flavia was raising the lamp to light one of the torches, a running figure jostled her against Nubia.

"Oof!" cried Flavia. The bronze oil lamp clattered to the floor, and darkness swallowed them.

Flavia groped for her lamp on the oily wooden floor. She could hear Tigris barking, the shutter still banging, and more footsteps running. A dim light flared, illuminating the dark corridor to their left. Flavia saw Jonathan holding his oil lamp to a torch in its angled wall bracket. As the flames took hold, the golden light in the corridor grew brighter. Tigris ran toward the girls. He wagged his tail at them and began lapping the pooled olive oil from Flavia's lamp.

"What's happening?" asked Jonathan, coming up with his lamp. Lupus was behind him. He had taken the flaming torch from its bracket.

A man's cry made all four of them turn. Tigris skittered down the corridor in the direction of the cry, and Lupus hurried after him, his torch crackling. Flavia and her two friends followed. Rounding a corner, Flavia found Lupus and Tigris standing in the doorway of her father's two-room suite. Lupus had pulled aside the heavy curtain, and the flickering light from his torch illuminated a little reception room with cream and red frescoed walls. Against the right-hand wall was a small table with a tiny nightlight burning. In the left-hand wall was a dark doorway leading to her father's inner bedroom. In the center of this reception room was a dining couch made up as a bed. Aristo stood behind this couch, bent over the figure stretched out on it.

"What?" cried Flavia, pushing past Lupus. "What is it, Aristo—?"

Then she saw the figure on the bed, and the words died on her lips.

It was a sight Flavia would never forget, one that would haunt her dreams for many years to come.

Her father lay on his back, asleep. He was pale as ivory and perfectly still. Then Aristo raised his head and she saw a look of horrified disbelief twist his handsome features as he looked at her, and then down at the bloody knife in his hand.

Flavia suddenly knew with a terrible certainty that her father was not asleep.

10

SCROLL III

"Pater!" Flavia screamed and took a step toward the figure on the bed. Then she stopped. Once, in Ostia, she had seen a row of ivory statues waiting to be tinted. With his eyes closed and the covers down around his waist, her father was as still and pale as one of those statues. In the flickering light of torch and lamp, she could see no mark on his face, but his fair hair was matted with something dark. The wind moaned in the eaves outside the room, and a draft made the torches flicker.

Now Aristo was staring in horror at the front of his unbelted white tunic. It was stained as red as the cloak draped over his shoulders.

Tigris moved forward to sniff at a pool of some dark liquid beneath the bed near a pair of sandals; then he started to lap at it.

When Flavia saw what Tigris was lapping, a choking nausea rose up and filled her throat so that the only release was for her to open her mouth and scream. A moment later she felt the room darken and tilt and swallow her up.

Nubia caught Flavia as she fainted, and a moment later she heard another scream.

As Jonathan pulled Tigris away from under the bed, Helen, the landlady, pushed into the room. Two of her house slaves followed behind, carrying torches.

"What have you done to Marcus?" Helen screamed, bending over Flavia's father. She looked down at him and then up at Aristo, who remained silent.

"You've killed him! You've stabbed a defenseless man in his sleep. Fortunatus! Syriacus! Seize him!"

As the two big house slaves put their torches in wall brackets and moved cautiously toward Aristo, he dropped the knife and took a step back, shaking his head.

"Get him!" shrieked Helen to her slaves. "Don't let him escape!"

The Syrian slave seized Aristo while the other wrenched his hands behind his back. "Throw me that curtain tie, boy!" he said to Jonathan. "Quickly!"

Jonathan pulled a green cord from its brass hook behind the door curtain and tossed it to the slave. Aristo did not seem to notice the slave tying his wrists behind him and then knotting his cloak in front, so that he was doubly bound. He was staring toward the doorway of the room, as if he saw something terrible standing there.

Nubia followed his gaze, but the doorway was empty.

Flavia groaned and stirred in Nubia's arms.

"Get him out of here!" cried Helen. "Take him to the vigiles at Cenchrea. By the gods he'll pay for this! Oh, Marcus! Marcus!" She reached a hand toward Flavia's father but could not bring herself to touch the body. She began to sob hysterically.

The slaves pushed Aristo roughly around the couch to the door, and one of them took Lupus's torch. As they passed, Aristo turned his head to look at the girls. Flavia was moaning, her eyes still closed, so she did not see his expression. But Nubia did.

She saw a mixture of horror and disbelief in his eyes, and something else that she could not identify. He opened his mouth—perhaps to say something to her—but already Helen's slaves had shoved him through the doorway and he was gone.

Lupus took a step toward the body on the couch.

Around him it was chaos. Guests and their slaves were crowding the doorway, wanting to see the body. Jonathan had taken Tigris back to their room, and Lupus could hear his muffled barks of protest. Flavia was conscious but she was still slumped on the floor, sobbing uncontrollably in Nubia's arms. The landlady, Helen, had begun to wail and tear her hair, too, and the red-haired slave girl had taken up the shrill ululation. Even the wind seemed to bemoan the brutal murder.

Lupus ignored the commotion and stared at the figure on the bed. He was surprised at how calm he felt. Three years before, when he was only six, he had seen his own father lying dead in a pool of blood. But Flavia's father did not look dead. He looked as if he was sleeping. In the flickering torchlight it was hard to tell that his tunic was stained red with blood, not dye.

On an impulse, Lupus took another step closer and pressed his hand to the dead man's throat, as he had sometimes seen Jonathan's father do. To his surprise he found the body was still quite warm. Lupus's heart gave a kick.

He turned and grunted urgently toward Flavia. She was still sitting on the floor, lost in her grief, but Jonathan had just pushed his way back into the crowded room. When he saw Lupus beckoning, he came at once.

Lupus watched Jonathan rest his head on the captain's chest. Abruptly, he straightened up and looked wide-eyed at Lupus, who nodded vigorously.

"Flavia!" cried Jonathan, shouting to make himself heard above the wails of the women and the excited babble of the men. "He's alive!"

Apart from the moaning of the wind, the room was suddenly silent.

"He's not dead! He's alive," repeated Jonathan angrily. "But he won't be for long if we don't get help. I can barely hear his heart-beat."

Flavia lifted her tear-streaked face in disbelief. Then she was on her feet.

"Pater!" she cried, going to the couch. "Oh, Pater! Help him! Get a doctor!"

Helen, the landlady, bent over the bed, too. Her dark hair had come partly unpinned, and there were smears of dark kohl beneath her slanting eyes, but now she turned to the red-haired slave girl. "Persis, I think one of the guests is a doctor," she cried. "The old man downstairs in the Ariadne suite."

"I'll bring him, domina," said the girl, and pushed through the excited throng of guests jostling to see the victim.

"Hurry!" cried Flavia after her. "Oh, please hurry!"

Helen, the landlady, and the red-haired slave girl had cleared the small room of guests. They had brought in a twelve-wick bronze standing lamp and two more wall torches to light the bedroom. As the doctor began to examine Flavia's father, Jonathan stepped closer to watch. The doctor—an old man with gray hair and a wispy beard—had cut the captain's tunic and peeled back the bloody cloth to examine his chest and arms.

"Three of these wounds are fairly superficial," the doctor murmured in Latin, "but this one above the heart by the collarbone is bad. Also, he's lost a lot of blood; the mattress is fairly soaked with it. I don't know if . . ." He lifted his head and looked at Helen. "I don't think it would be wise to bleed him." Jonathan stared at the doctor. He knew that most doctors resorted to bleeding as a matter of course, but in this case that would be madness.

"My assistant isn't back yet," said the doctor to Helen, "so I'll need someone to go and find some cobwebs. I'll also need someone to hold the wounds shut while I sew them up. Oh, and bring me a sea sponge soaked in vinegar," he added.

"Get a bowl of vinegar," said Helen to Persis, "and the sea sponge from my bedroom dressing table."

The doctor called something after the girl in Greek and then spoke to Flavia in Latin. "You're his daughter, aren't you? Will you help me wash his wounds?"

Flavia did not reply. Jonathan saw a look of horror on her face.

"Nubia, why don't *you* sponge the wounds?" he said, and turned to Flavia. "You go find some cobwebs."

Flavia nodded and wandered out of the room in a daze.

"Go with her, Lupus," said Jonathan, and turned back to the doctor. "I can assist you," he said. "My father's a doctor, and I've helped him before."

The doctor stared at him for a moment, then gave a curt nod. Up close, Jonathan could see particles of food in his beard.

Lupus followed Flavia out of the room, and a moment later Helen's slave girl returned with a sea sponge floating in a ceramic bowl of vinegar. She set the bowl down on the small table beside the wall, then carried the table to the bedside. The doctor was showing Nubia the wounds that needed sponging. There were two gashes on the captain's left arm, one on his left side, and a wound in his chest, above the heart. The slave girl gasped.

"Your name is Persis, isn't it?" Jonathan said to her.

The girl nodded, not taking her eyes from the captain's wounds.

"Could you bring a bowl of warm water, Persis?" asked Jonathan.

15

As Persis nodded and backed out of the room, Jonathan turned to the doctor. "My father always washes his hands before he works."

The doctor glared at him, but when Persis brought in the bowl a few moments later, he broke off trying to thread a bronze needle in order to wash his hands.

Lupus and Flavia reappeared in the doorway. Lupus stepped into the room and carefully wiped his ball of cobwebs on the doctor's leather instrument pouch. He ran off to look for more, but Flavia lingered near the doorway, a dazed look on her face.

Jonathan had just dried his hands on the linen towel draped over the slave girl's arm when he heard the doctor curse in Greek. The man was still struggling with needle and thread.

"Here, let me," said Nubia, and deftly threaded the needle.

The doctor grunted his thanks, and indicated the first wound to Nubia, the one on the captain's chest. When she had gently sponged it, he placed some cobwebs into the open wound and indicated that Jonathan should push the edges of the flesh together. Then he took the threaded needle and began to sew. On the bloody mattress, Captain Geminus stirred and groaned softly. Flavia made a strange choking noise and ran out of the room, followed by Helen and Persis.

Jonathan heard Nubia take a deep breath, and he glanced up at her. Was she going to bolt, too?

She looked up from sponging the wound, her eyes golden in the lamplight, and she gave a small nod in response to his encouraging smile. Then they returned to their work, and from that moment Jonathan lost track of time.

They found Flavia in the purple twilight before dawn.

She was lying on one of the dining couches out in the garden. Helen rose from the foot of the couch when the three friends

16

came through the ivy arch. A crescent moon touched the tops of the pines to the east, and somewhere in the distance a cock was crowing. The wind had died.

"She wouldn't go back inside," said Helen, "so I got Persis to bring her some blankets and a cup of hot wine." She looked at Jonathan, and he saw her eyes were swollen from weeping. "How is Marcus?" she asked.

Jonathan sat on the couch opposite and sighed. "Still unconscious. We cleaned his wounds and put cobwebs inside and sewed them up. The doctor says he needs to rest in a quiet place for a week or two and that he must not travel."

Helen nodded. "Now that you've finished, I'll have my slaves move him down to my private triclinium. It's the quietest room in the inn and looks out onto the herb garden." She looked toward the lavender sky in the east. "I'd better get the slaves to clean up all that blood." She sighed. "Why don't you go back up to your rooms and get some sleep?"

"May we stay here with our friend?" asked Nubia.

"Of course," said Helen. "I'll send a girl with some more blankets, and I'll make sure you're undisturbed. Unless something happens," she added, and Jonathan saw fresh tears fill her eyes as she turned away.

As he watched her weave her way out of the dim garden, he felt the brand on his left shoulder throb painfully, as it always did when he was tired. His eyes felt gritty and his right ear tickled. He rubbed it and recoiled when he saw the dried blood on his fingers. It must have come from when he had rested his head against Captain Geminus's chest, to listen for the heartbeat. He glanced at his friends. Nubia had stretched out beside Flavia. Lupus was curled up on the central couch, his knees drawn up to his chin and his eyes already closed.

Jonathan bent and dipped his hands in the cold water of the ornamental pool and washed his face and ears. When he rose up, dripping, he saw Persis placing three folded blankets on the end of Lupus's couch. She gave him a sad smile and ran back toward the inn. Jonathan spread a blanket over Lupus and took one for himself and lay down on the remaining couch.

As soon as he closed his eyes he saw an image of Aristo standing over the captain's body.

He opened his eyes. "Why did you do it, Aristo?" he whispered. Immediately another image came into his head: Aristo in the woods outside Ostia, bending to cut off an ostrich's head with a single clean stroke of his knife, a sharp iron blade with a bronze boar's-head handle.

The knife! Aristo had dropped it on the bedroom floor, and nobody had bothered to pick it up.

Another cock began crowing nearby as Jonathan pushed off the blanket and ran back through the ivy arch into the colonnaded courtyard and up the stairs. He found Helen overseeing the cleanup of the Orpheus room. Persis and a fair-haired slave girl had pushed the bed and candelabra against the wall, next to the small table with the night-light. They were on their hands and knees, drying the varnished wooden floor.

Helen looked up eagerly as Jonathan came in. "Oh," she said, and her face fell, "I thought it was Fortunatus and Syriacus coming back."

Jonathan needed a moment to catch his breath. "The knife," he said. "Aristo dropped his knife. Have you found it?"

Helen frowned and said something to the slaves in Greek.

They tipped their heads back in the Greek manner, and one of them held up the bloody sandals.

"These sandals are the only thing they found on the floor," said Helen.

Jonathan went to the doorway of the room that led off from the Orpheus room. "What's in here?" he asked, taking a torch from its bracket and looking in. It was a small room with black walls and frescoes of sea nymphs. It had two small windows but no other entry or exit. There was barely enough room for a low bed, a cedarwood chest, an oak table, and a bronze and leather armchair.

"That's where Marcus sleeps," said Helen. "He likes this room because it's quiet."

"But you have to go through the Orpheus room to get out," said Jonathan. "Didn't he mind the lack of privacy? Didn't it disturb him when people stayed here?"

"The Orpheus room is actually part of a suite," said Helen. "Flavia requested it for Aristo, because of the frescoes. Your tutor was only going to be here for one night, and Marcus said he didn't mind sharing. So we moved the table and chair in here from the Orpheus room, and we brought a dining couch in there for Aristo to sleep on."

"Interesting," murmured Jonathan. "So nobody has come in or out of this room since the attack?"

"Nobody," said Helen. "I'm sure of it."

"I'm going to have a quick look for the knife, if you don't mind."

"Of course not."

Jonathan fixed the torch in a bracket on the wall of the inner room and opened the bronze shutters of both windows. The windows faced east, and a pearly predawn light flooded the room, making it easier for him to see. On top of the cedarwood chest was the captain's cord belt and money pouch and beside the bed his red leather sandals. Among the writing things on the table was a knife. It was a souvenir Flavia had brought her father from Rome two months before, a folding knife with an iron blade and a bronze handle in the shape of a gladiator. But this was obviously not the weapon used to stab the captain; its blade was shorter than Jonathan's thumb.

"Nothing?" said Helen, seeing the expression on his face as he emerged from the bedroom.

Jonathan shook his head. "I don't suppose it matters," he said. "It's not as if it's a clue to a mystery."

"No," said Helen wearily. "There's no mystery about who tried to kill Marcus."

"The mystery," murmured Jonathan as he turned to go, "is why."

SCROLL IV

"Flavia. Flavia, my dear. Please wake up. Something's happened."
An accented woman's voice and a hand gently shaking Flavia's
shoulder.

Flavia opened her eyes, and for an instant she was aware of glorious sunlight illuminating bright green pine needles above her.
Birds were singing and she could hear doves cooing in their dove-
cote. Then the memory of the previous night's events came back
like a kick in the stomach. "Pater!" she cried, sitting up on the
couch. "Is Pater . . . ?"

"He's alive," said Helen quietly. "He's alive but he's in a very
deep sleep."

As Flavia stood up, a wave of nausea swept over her. She sank to
her hands and knees and was sick on the grass. Nubia knelt beside
her and held her head until Flavia had finished.

"What's happened?" asked Jonathan groggily from his couch.

"My two slaves have just returned," said Helen. "I'm afraid they
lost Aristo."

"What?" cried Flavia, looking up at Helen. The woman had
pinned up her long dark hair and put on a clean stola, but the
shadows under her slanting dark eyes made her look tired.

"Fortunatus and Syriacus were taking him to the vigiles at

Cenchrea," said Helen, "so that they could hold him until the authorities from Corinth could take over. But he escaped."

"How?" asked Flavia. She felt sick again.

"They think he had an accomplice. A woman. As they were leading him down the road, a woman screamed and Fortunatus went to her aid. He assumed she was being molested. Anyway, Aristo chose that moment to attack Syriacus. He knocked him to the ground, then kicked him senseless."

"Aristo did this thing?" asked Nubia.

"Even though his hands were tied?" Jonathan raised his eyebrows. "And his cloak knotted at the front?"

"Yes. Syriacus says he fought like a tiger, with the strength of ten men. When Syriacus recovered and Fortunatus returned, Aristo was gone. They tried to find him and they even went to his parents' house in Corinth but . . ." Helen shook her head. "I'm sorry, Flavia. He got away."

Flavia sat beside her father in the private triclinium of Helen's Hospitium. It was a small room, not much bigger than their own triclinium at home in Ostia, and it looked out onto a sheltered north-facing herb garden. A wooden latticework screen on rollers could be pulled across for privacy, but at the moment it was concertinaed against the left-hand edge of the wide doorway.

Her father lay on a couch placed against the central wall, beneath a fresco of a painted window looking out onto painted woods. On the two side walls were colorful frescoes of paths leading to round shrines, painted with such accurate perspective that at first glance they looked real. Shrubs had been painted in the foreground. On one of them—a rosebush in bloom—sat a nightingale, his beak open in silent song.

Flavia looked away from the painted bird to study her father's face. He was pale and although his breathing was steady, it was shallow and barely audible.

The light in the triclinium dimmed as Helen appeared in the wide doorway with two men.

"Flavia," she said. "I've brought Lucius Sergius Agaclytus, the best doctor in Corinth."

The taller of the two men had a face like a handsome monkey. But he had intelligent eyes and a quiet confidence.

"You're Flavia, the victim's daughter," he said in perfect Latin.

"Yes." She stood up and allowed him and his young assistant to approach the couch.

"I'm Agaclytus," he said, "and this is my assistant, Petros. When did this happen?"

"Last night," whispered Flavia. "Around midnight, I think."

Out of the corner of her eye she saw Helen nodding.

"How old is your father?" Agaclytus gently pulled back the blankets, and Flavia almost fainted when she saw the swollen, stitched wounds in the flesh of her father's chest and arm.

She looked away, toward one of the painted temples, and took a few deep breaths. "Pater will be thirty-two in a few weeks," she said.

"Who did this?"

"My tutor, Aristo," she said, feeling her eyes fill with tears. "He's been with us for three years. I don't know why he did it. I always thought he and Pater liked each other. . . ." Flavia trailed off, aware of the doctor bending, examining, lightly touching, murmuring in Greek to his assistant, who was taking notes on a wax tablet. Finally he pulled the blanket up to her father's neck and straightened again.

"He has lost a great deal of blood," said the doctor. "The stitching is rather clumsy but the wounds have been cleaned well and if they do not become corrupted he should live." He turned to Helen and said something in Greek. They had a rapid exchange, during which Helen kept glancing nervously at Flavia. The doctor shook his head sadly. Finally he turned his simian eyes on Flavia.

"According to the landlady here, your father did regain consciousness briefly at around the third hour this morning."

"He did?" Flavia jumped up and clapped her hands together.

Helen turned to Flavia. "I didn't tell you," she said, "because he didn't recognize me. He didn't even know where he was." Her dark eyes looked bruised with grief.

"That's not surprising," said Flavia to her. "We've only been here a few nights. We don't really know you that well, and Pater can be absentminded."

"Your father always stays here when he passes through Corinth," said Helen. She lifted her chin a fraction. "Marcus and I know each other very well. But today he kept asking for Myrtilla." Helen lowered her eyes. "Who is she, do you know?"

Flavia felt her stomach sink.

"Do you know who Myrtilla is?" asked the doctor.

"Myrtilla is—was my mother," said Flavia. "But she . . . she died when I was three . . . seven, no—nearly eight years ago."

"Your father might just be confused," said the doctor, "unless it's amnesia."

"What?"

"Amnesia." When he saw the blank look on her face, he said, "I'm sorry, that's a Greek word and I don't know if there is a Latin equivalent. It means a loss of memory. People with amnesia often completely forget events of recent years, but the past can seem like yesterday to them. It often happens to those who've had a blow to the head."

"But he didn't have a blow to the head," said Flavia. "He was stabbed."

"On the contrary. Do you see this lump here?" Agaclytus gently pushed away some light brown hair on the back of her father's head.

Flavia's eyes opened in horror. "Yes," she whispered, noticing for the first time a lump almost the size of a chicken's egg on her father's head.

"This is probably where he struck his head against the hard edge of the bed. That's why he was so still when you found him. Do you see these two bruises on his neck? Look. Right here at the base of the throat. This is where the attacker's thumbs pressed in."

Flavia had no words. She hadn't even noticed.

"But that means . . ." she whispered.

The doctor nodded grimly. "Not only did that young man stab your father, but it appears he slammed his head against the wooden bed frame and also tried to strangle him. There is no doubt that this Aristo was determined to see your father dead."

"Flavia?"

Flavia lifted her head to see four figures framed in the wide doorway of the triclinium. The green garden beyond them was flooded with brilliant noonday light, and she could not see their faces clearly.

"Flavia," said Jonathan, "may we come in?"

She nodded but put her finger to her lips.

Jonathan, Nubia, Lupus, and a gray-haired old man stepped into the small dining room and stood beside the bed. They gazed down at Captain Geminus, still sleeping deeply.

"How is he?" whispered the man. He had a cheerful tanned face and long frizzy gray hair tied back in a ponytail. His name was Atticus, and he was one of her father's sailors, a cook and carpenter.

"Pater is still asleep," said Flavia. "I want to be here when he wakes up."

Lupus was looking at the frescoed wall beside Flavia, with its realistic path leading to a small round temple. He waved good-bye, pretended to start down the painted path toward the temple, and feigned surprise when he banged into the wall. Flavia did not smile, and Lupus shrugged.

"Flavia," said Jonathan softly. "We've spoken to the doctor, Aga-clytus. He says it would be better if you kept yourself busy and let

Helen get on with nursing your father. He thinks you need some rest and distraction and—"

"No!" cried Flavia vehemently. "I'm not going to leave Pater! What will he do without me? If he wakes up and I'm not here, he'll be lost. I'm not leaving him alone so Aristo can come back and finish the job tonight!"

"Helen's slaves can guard your father," said Jonathan.

"Besides, I wouldn't worry about young Aristo trying to kill your father again," said Atticus. "He was seen early this morning running down the road to Athens."

Flavia looked up. "Someone saw him? Did they catch him?"

"Flavia." Jonathan took a step closer. "It's just like in Rome. The vigiles won't bother going after him. They just don't have the time or the money. This is a private matter. If we want to bring Aristo to justice, we'll either have to hire someone or do it ourselves. The three of us have discussed it—" here Nubia and Lupus nodded "—and we think we should do it ourselves. Helen says she'll give us a carriage and four mules. Atticus has agreed to come with us," added Jonathan, glancing at the gray-haired Greek. "He can be our translator and bodyguard."

"Your guide, too," said Atticus. "I grew up in Athens, and I know the road from here to there. We'll catch him."

"Will you come with us?" Jonathan asked Flavia.

"No," she said.

"But don't you want to catch Aristo?" said Jonathan. "Don't you want justice to be done?"

Flavia was silent.

"Flavia," said Nubia, "we need you for the clues. You are good at this."

Lupus nodded.

"Did you ever think," said Jonathan, "that maybe all the mysteries you've solved so far have been training for just such a time as this?"

"No!" said Flavia again. "I can't leave Pater. You go if you like. But don't ask me to abandon him!" She hid her face in her hands. Everything seemed unreal: the room with its painted garden, the unfamiliar birdsong outside, the smell of pine cones burning on an altar somewhere.

Even the man in the bed seemed strange, unlike her father. Surely this was a nightmare and she would wake from it soon. As hot tears welled up and spilled over, she surrendered herself to weeping. When she finally looked up again, the room was silent and the bright green square of the doorway stood empty.

Flavia was dreaming. She stood in a dark, smoky atrium before an alabaster lararium. In the shrine were little statues, the lares and penates of the household, and a bronze snake for luck. Suddenly the little figures began to tremble and whimper with fear. Now Flavia could hear what was frightening them. Terrible iron footsteps coming up the stairs. The snake writhed in terror, and the little gods scrambled over each other to hide at the back of the shrine. The slow footsteps were coming closer, shaking the whole house now, and Flavia turned with horror to see who—or what— they were.

Her head jerked up, and she blinked at the bright afternoon light. Where was she? In Greece, in a painted triclinium with her father on the couch beside her, unconscious.

No, he wasn't unconscious! His eyes were open, and he was frowning up at the blue-painted ceiling with a look of heartbreaking confusion on his face.

"Pater," she cried. "You're awake!" She almost threw her arms around his neck, but she saw a look of alarm flit across his features.

"Don't worry, Pater," she said. "I won't touch your wounds."

"Who are you?" he asked, his voice barely more than a whisper.

"What?"

"Where's Myrtilla?"

"Pater, it's me. Flavia. Aristo stabbed you, but you're going to be all right."

"Why . . . why are you calling me Pater?"

"Pater, it's me. Flavia. Your daughter. Don't you remember me?"

"Please, little girl, try to find Myrtilla. Or my brother. His name is Gaius Flavius Geminus. You must find them. The ship sails for Alexandria tomorrow."

"Shhh," whispered Flavia, fighting tears. "Don't try to get up. You're badly wounded. Rest your head back on the pillow. That's right. I'll try to find Myrtilla or Gaius."

"Thank you," the words were barely audible and his eyes were closing again. "Thank you. You're a good girl."

"Have you finished it yet?" asked Jonathan.

Lupus stood hunched over a small table in the boys' room. He shook his head impatiently, and without looking up from his work he made a dismissive flapping motion with his left hand. Jonathan sighed and wandered over to Nubia. She had laid out their things on one of the beds and was now packing the most essential items. Helen had given them three travelers' knapsacks.

Finally Lupus grunted and stepped back from the table. Jonathan and Nubia both hurried over. On the table before Lupus lay a wax tablet, like a small wooden booklet. The two inner leaves were coated with a thin layer of yellow beeswax, which could be marked with a stylus. But Jonathan and Nubia were not looking at the inside. They were looking at the back of the tablet, where Lupus had painted a portrait of Aristo in colored wax on the smooth wood.

"Oh Lupus," breathed Nubia, "it is a wonderful likeness."

Jonathan gave a low whistle of approval. "That's brilliant, Lupus. That should certainly help us find him."

"How soon can we leave?" came a voice from the doorway.

Jonathan and the others looked up to see Flavia standing there.

"You've decided to come with us?" He raised his eyebrows.

She nodded. "Can we leave right now?"

Jonathan glanced at the others. "We were going to leave tomorrow at first light."

"I want to go now. Right now," said Flavia. "We don't have a moment to lose."

"But Flavia," said Nubia. "In five or six hours sun will set, and then it will be most difficult to travel."

Lupus nodded his agreement.

"Besides," said Jonathan, "Atticus has gone to Corinth to try to get some more information about Aristo, in case there have been any more sightings of him. We can't go without him. He's going to be our bodyguard and translator."

Nubia stood up and took a hesitant step toward Flavia.

"How is your pater?" she asked.

"Pater just woke up," said Flavia, "and he didn't recognize me. He doesn't even know who I am."

Nubia was about to run to her friend to comfort her, but the look on Flavia's face stopped her.

"We're going to find Aristo," said Flavia grimly, "and when we do, I'm going to make him pay for what he did to Pater!"

SCROLL V

As Nubia pressed her heels into Caltha's flank, the mare broke into a canter. That was better. It felt good to be in control of something. She felt Flavia's arms tight around her waist. That felt good, too. For once she was the leader, not Flavia.

Despite her anguish for Aristo and for Flavia's father, Nubia could not suppress the joy flooding her heart as the horse clopped along the winding dirt road toward Corinth. It was a glorious day, warm and fragrant with the clean, pungent scent of pine trees and the sea. Above the steady clip-clop of Caltha's hooves she could hear birds whistling their appreciation of the spring sunshine. On her left, the Acrocorinth rose dramatically, a small mountain against the deep blue sky. As they passed pedestrians, mule carts, and other riders, Nubia smiled inwardly at their whistles of admiration or cries of greeting.

Beyond the tombs that lined the road on both left and right, she caught glimpses of green cypress trees and red-roofed temples and gilded statues in the sanctuaries. The craggy Acrocorinth was still looming, but it changed shape slightly as the road circled its base.

Finally they reached the cypress grove called Craneum and the triumphal arch topped by a gilded chariot that marked the entrance to Corinth. Nubia did not pass through the arch, but guided Caltha to the right, along the road that led down through the vineyards to Corinth's western port, Lechaeum. It still felt awkward using reins, but the mare seemed to understand the pressure of Nubia's heels on her flanks.

They passed beneath the shadow of a twenty-foot statue of the sea god, Poseidon, standing above a fountain. As they descended the last mile to sea level, the road became a covered colonnade cut into the hillside. It was cool and shaded here, but noisy because the sound of Caltha's hooves echoed off the stone wall.

"It's just like the road down to the Villa Limona," said Flavia in Nubia's ear.

Nubia nodded and pulled Caltha up beside a white stuccoed column to let an oxcart pass. Presently they emerged from the echoing colonnade into sunshine and relative silence. A few minutes later they rode beneath the arch marking the port of Lechaeum.

A cluster of warehouses and cauponas surrounded the docks but gave way on either side to a gray shingle beach dotted with gorse and scrubby grasses. Beyond lay the Gulf of Corinth, gleaming like a vast shield of beaten silver, with the hazy blue mountains of the mainland rising beyond it.

Nubia urged Caltha down toward the docks. At once her sharp eyes spotted the *Delphina*'s mast rising among others. Caltha's hoofbeats took on a hollow ring as they rode along a wooden pier. Their arrival at the *Delphina*'s berth was greeted by a chorus of good-humored catcalls from sailors in the surrounding boats.

Nubia lifted her chin a fraction and ignored them. She pulled up Caltha, swung her right leg over the horse's neck, and let herself slip down the mare's damp flank onto the pier. It was farther than it looked and although the landing jarred her from heel to chin, she acted as if everything was fine and reached her arms up to Flavia.

"Oh, no," said Flavia. "I'm not doing what you just did. It's too far. It feels as if I'm miles up!"

"Don't worry, Miss Flavia," said a man's voice, curiously light. "I'll help you!"

"Punicus!" cried Flavia, and Nubia turned to see the *Delphina*'s helmsman coming down the gangplank. He was a big, muscular man with a bald head and light brown skin. The other crew member—a young man from Cnidos named Alexandros—waved cheerfully from the stern platform.

When Punicus reached the dock, he lifted Flavia down and then greeted both girls with a gap-toothed grin.

"Punicus, we don't have a moment to lose," said Flavia. "You heard what happened to Pater?"

The Phoenician's grin instantly faded and he nodded. "Atticus just left. He told us you're going to try to catch the culprit."

"That's right," said Flavia. "But we need money. Lots of it. Is Pater's strongbox on board?"

"Of course. Down in the hold," he lowered his voice to a whisper. "In its usual secret hiding place."

"Good," said Flavia, starting up the gangplank. "Here's what I want you to do—Oh, Nubia!" she said, turning back. "Wait here with the horse. I'll only be a few moments."

Nubia nodded and sighed. With Flavia, she was never the leader for long.

Two hours later, back at Helen's Hospitium, Flavia looked up from her wax tablet as she heard hooves on the fine gravel drive that led to the inn's main entrance.

"Atticus! At last! Where have you been?"

Brown hens had been pecking on the gravel approach to the inn. Now they scattered as Atticus swung himself off the mule and handed the reins to one of Helen's slaves.

"What's happened?" said the old sailor. "The captain! He's not . . . is he—?"

32

"He's conscious," said Flavia, and took a deep breath to stop the tears from coming again. "But he doesn't remember me. He has something called amnesia."

Atticus shook his gray head. "Thank the gods he's still alive," he said. "But amnesia, that's bad. I knew someone who had that once. He never recovered because they couldn't find the curse tablet." Atticus spat and made the sign against evil.

"I knew it!" cried Flavia, clenching her fist. "That's what Helen said. She said Aristo probably cursed my father and unless we undo the curse he'll never remember who he is!" She shook her head. "I knew that doctor was wrong. How can a bump on the head make you forget?"

"Not likely," said Atticus. "Have you looked for a strip of lead nailed to a doorpost?"

"Yes," said Flavia. "Helen's slaves have searched everywhere: all the doorposts both inside and out. All the columns and walls and trees in the garden. They even looked in the cistern."

"He could have hidden it anywhere," said Atticus grimly. "Even buried it! And if he used a curse nail we'll never find it."

"That's why we have to go now! We'll catch him and force him to tell us where the curse is. Did you find out anything in town?"

"I did. The name of a woman who thinks she saw him."

"Tell me!"

"Name's Aphrodite. She's a farmer's widow. Lives beyond Isthmia, on the Athens Road. Early this morning she went out to feed her pigs and saw a man sleeping at the foot of a poplar tree near the road. She went toward him, and when he stood up she saw that he was bound and that he wore a bloodstained tunic. According to her, he ran off toward Athens."

"If his hands are still tied," said Flavia, "it will make it harder for him to move fast. I think we should go now. Every minute we waste could make a difference."

"But Miss Flavia, it will be dark in a few hours." The late afternoon sun illuminated Atticus's round face, shiny as a chestnut and almost as brown.

"I've calculated he's had a seventeen-hour start," said Flavia, holding up her wax tablet. "Let's not give him any more advantage." The brown hens pecking at her feet clucked and flapped for the shrubs as Tigris bounded out of the inn and down the steps. Flavia's three friends followed, their footsteps crunching on the gravel. "Is everything ready?" she asked them.

They nodded.

"I have packed essential belongings," said Nubia.

"I've got some maps and guides," said Jonathan, and tapped the quiver over his shoulder. "Plus my bow and arrows."

Lupus held up five water gourds in one hand and the wax tablet with Aristo's portrait in the other.

Flavia turned back to Atticus. "Did you know that Helen has given us her best carruca and four mules? She said we could have them. Sell them, eat them, anything . . ."

Atticus whistled under his breath. "That is very generous. She must really like your father," he said.

"Flavia!" said Jonathan, holding up a pair of red leather sandals. "Look what Nubia just found: Aristo's sandals."

"Those belong to Aristo?"

Nubia nodded. "But it is strange," she said, "because I find them in your father's bedroom, the room with gray sea nymphs on a black wall, next to the Orpheus room."

"You're absolutely sure they're Aristo's?" asked Flavia.

Nubia nodded. "I am sure."

"Excellent," said Flavia.

Atticus scratched his woolly gray hair. "What good are Aristo's sandals?"

"First of all," said Flavia, "it tells us he's not only bound but barefoot, which will slow him down. But more importantly," she said, bending to give Tigris a pat, "it means our best tracker can easily follow his scent!"

"According to this book," said Jonathan, "we're traveling the same route Theseus took when he went to Athens to claim his birthright."

It was early evening. They had made an offering for a good hunt at an ancient shrine of Artemis, and almost immediately Tigris had found Aristo's scent on the side of the Athens Road, which passed between vineyards and pine trees on the left and the blue sea on the right.

Helen's four-wheeled carruca was made of oak and wicker, light and strong. It had spoked wheels and a bucket of grease hanging from the rear axle. There were padded benches along each side, with storage space underneath. At each of the four corners were sockets for the posts of the awning by day, or torches for night travel. The unbleached linen awning was up now, and the carruca rumbled after Tigris at a steady pace. The grinding of the wooden wheels and the clopping hooves of four mules gave their quest a sense of rhythmic urgency.

"What book is that?" said Flavia, who was sitting beside Atticus at the front.

Jonathan held it up. "It's called *A Guide to Corinth, Attica, and Boeotia*. Helen said I could borrow it."

"Let me see," said Flavia, reaching back.

"It does not look like a book," said Nubia. "It resembles a wax tablet."

"It's a cross between a wax tablet and a scroll," said Jonathan. "It has leaves, like a wax tablet, but they're made of papyrus not wood."

"It's called a codex," said Flavia, flipping through the papyrus pages. "Pater has some in his library. His are mainly poetry. . . ." She handed the book back to Jonathan.

Jonathan raised his eyebrows in surprise. Flavia usually confiscated any new book he showed her and kept it until she'd read it.

"It's good, Flavia," he said. "It has all the landmarks and the legends behind them, and it even recommends good hotels and taverns. The best places to stay—like Helen's Hospitium—are marked with a little house with a courtyard. The decent ones get two little towers, and the ones that just scrape by only get one tower."

Flavia gave him a distracted nod over her shoulder.

"Also," he continued, "this book tells you all the places where Theseus performed his exploits."

"I know who Theseus is," said Nubia. "He is the hero in myth who conquers the man-bull. He does this on an island far away from here."

"That's right," said Atticus. "The monster was called the Minotaur, and it lived on Crete. I was in Crete once a few years ago. You can still see the actual labyrinth."

"Theseus had some adventures before he fought the Minotaur," said Jonathan. "According to this guidebook, he had to lift a big rock to discover his birthright. He tried to lift it every year and when he was fifteen he finally did it. Underneath he found a pair of gold leather sandals and a sword that had belonged to his father, Aegeus, the King of Athens. So he set out to claim his birthright. But instead of going to Athens the easy way—by ship—he decided to take the land route, which was full of murderers and monsters. He wanted his father to be proud of him."

"Maybe we should go by ship," said Nubia, "to be arriving in Athens before Aristo."

"That would be a good idea if we were certain he was headed for Athens," said Flavia, "but although they call this the Athens Road it leads to other places. Right, Atticus?"

"Correct," he replied. He had wrapped the reins around his leather wristbands.

Jonathan looked up from the guidebook at some bushy green pines scrolling past on either side of the road. "It might have been somewhere around here," he said, "that Theseus met Sinis the Pine-Bender."

"Why do they call him Pine-Bender?" asked Nubia.

Lupus grunted and stood up in the carriage. When he had their attention, he stretched out his arms and legs to make an X shape, wobbling a little as the carruca rocked. Then he twitched violently as if pulled from one side to the other, uttered a blood-curdling scream, and fell to the wooden floor.

"What is it?" cried Nubia.

Jonathan snorted. "Lupus was just demonstrating Sinis's *modus operandi*. He would catch helpless travelers, rob them, and then kill them in a horrible way. First he would bend a pine tree on one side of the road and tie one arm and leg to its top. Then he would bend a pine tree from the other side of the road and tie their other arm and leg, and when he simultaneously let the two pine trees go—"

Lupus opened his eyes, sat up, and nodded enthusiastically.

"—they would be torn in two, right down the middle!"

"Oh!" cried Nubia, covering her ears with her hands. "That is terrible!"

Jonathan nodded. "They must have been tall pines," he said, "not these bushy ones. . . . Oh, look there! Like those. Those are tall and flexible."

He bent his head over the book again. "The village of Cromyon is around here, too. That's where Theseus met the man-eating sow—"

"What is sow?" asked Nubia.

"Female pig," said Flavia.

"After he killed the man-eating sow," said Jonathan, "Theseus vanquished Sciron, another robber, who pushed travelers off a cliff to the sea below, where his man-eating pet turtle would finish them off. Then there was Procrustes, an innkeeper with a special bed. If you were too short for this special bed, he stretched your arms and legs out of their sockets to make you longer. On the other hand, if you were too tall—"

Lupus stood up again and made chopping motions.

"—he would chop off your feet."

"Top of your head, too, if necessary," said Atticus with a chuckle.

"Don't worry, Nubia," said Flavia, twisting around on her seat and looking down at them. "They're just myths."

Jonathan nodded. "I don't think we'll meet any ax-wielding innkeepers, and there's no such thing as a man-eating sow."

SCROLL VI

"Are you certain there is not such a thing as a man-eating sow?" said Nubia, pointing straight ahead.

They had passed the sanctuary of Isthmia, with its theater and white marble race course visible between a row of pines, and the sun was low in the west as they approached a farmhouse set back from the side of the road. The plaster had been white once, but now it was gray and peeling. If it had not been for half a dozen chickens pecking in the dust around it, Lupus would have thought the building abandoned. Between the road and the farmhouse was a muddy fenced enclosure. Lupus could see a shaven-headed slave boy throwing slops to several huge creatures on the other side of the wooden fence. The creatures in the pen were enormous pigs.

Tigris had run ahead to investigate these strange creatures, but now he backed off, tail between his legs.

Atticus reined in the mules with a click of his tongue. As they all piled out of the carruca, the slave boy looked at them in alarm, and then ran toward the house.

Lupus was the first to reach the pen. He uttered a low whistle. The pigs were huge. They were big as donkeys, though their legs were far shorter.

They all stood in silence for a few moments, watching the pigs snort and squeal as they fought over their slops.

"You know," remarked Atticus, "I've heard there really are man-eating pigs. They develop a taste for human flesh. Throw a corpse in there and they'll eat it all up."

"Ugh!" said Flavia.

"I wonder," mused Jonathan, "what would happen if you put a live but wounded person in the pen with pigs used to eating human flesh?"

"Jonathan! What a horrible thought!" said Flavia. "Being eaten alive by an enormous pig."

At that moment, a sturdy old woman came swaying up the dirt path from the house. She wore a greasy apron over a voluminous rust-colored stola, and her gray hair was twisted around a polished cow horn. She held a hunk of brown bread in one hand.

"You must be Atticus," she said in accented Latin. "You've been asking about me. I'm Aphrodite." She stopped and looked Flavia up and down. "I'd guess you're the murdered man's daughter."

"He's not dead!" cried Flavia.

"That's not what I've heard." Aphrodite tore at her bread with hard, toothless gums. "People say he was stabbed and strangled and finally beaten to death by a jealous husband."

"What?" cried Flavia and looked at her friends in horror. "WHAT? No! That's not what happened at all. There's no jealous husband, and Pater's not dead." She took a deep breath and tried to keep her voice calm. "But he is badly wounded and it seems he can't remember anything from the past eight years."

"Oh dear." The old lady spat in the dust and made the sign against evil. "Sounds to me like a curse."

"Yes," cried Flavia, "and unless we find the man who did it we'll never reverse it."

"Sorry I didn't grab him when I had the chance," said the old woman, looking wistful.

"Were you that close?" asked Jonathan.

"I was." The woman gestured with her piece of bread. "I was checking on my swine and I saw a flash of red and white over there. Under that poplar, where your black dog is sniffing. The white was his tunic fluttering in the breeze, and the red was a cloak bunched up around his neck. He looked like Adonis, fast asleep and waiting for his Aphrodite." She chuckled. "But his Aphrodite obviously wasn't *me*. When I came closer he jumped up and looked around, all trapped and wild, like a weasel in a wine press. It was then I noticed he was barefoot and that his wrists were tied behind him."

"I hear you chased him off," said Atticus.

"Not quite!" She laughed. "We stood staring at each other for a few moments. Then he went haring off down the road, his bare feet slapping and his legs pumping. . . . Nice legs," she added. "Muscular but not too thick."

There was a moment's silence, broken only by a bird's trill and Tigris's steady barking from the foot of the poplar tree.

Suddenly Lupus remembered his portrait of Aristo. He stepped forward, extending his wax tablet.

"What's this?" Aphrodite took the tablet and her beady eyes widened as she saw the portrait on the back. "Oh, yes," she gave a wheezing chuckle. "That's him all right. That's my sleeping Adonis."

Jonathan looked around with interest as the carriage rattled over the deep ruts in the stone *diolkos*. He had been here twice before. The first time a month previously, when the ship *Delphina* had been transported from west to east, and the second time only a few days ago, when she had been rolled back to the Gulf of Corinth. On both occasions the *diolkos* had been swarming with slaves and ships and wagons. Now it was almost deserted, though he heard a splash and the cries of men off to his right. It was dusk, and the last ship of the day had just crossed over the isthmus.

"Say good-bye to civilization," said Atticus, as they regained the dirt road.

"What?" said Jonathan.

"We're leaving the Roman world," said Atticus, "and we're about to enter the Greek one."

"What do you mean, Atticus?" Flavia frowned. "We've been in Greece for weeks."

"The *diolkos* marks the limit of Colonia Corinthiensis and of Roman influence," said Atticus. "I don't suppose you even noticed how many people speak Latin back there." Atticus chuckled as they shook their heads. "Half the people who live in Corinth are of Roman descent, or Phrygian, or Jewish. But that," he lifted his chin toward the landscape before them, "that's proper Greece. Land of sheep and goats, brigands and robbers, and disreputable guesthouses."

"Why didn't you tell us that before?" said Flavia.

"Don't you worry, Miss Flavia. Atticus is here to take care of you. And Flora, too."

Jonathan looked down at the object Atticus was patting. "You call your sword 'Flora'?"

"She's just a dagger," said Atticus with a grin. "Though I did name her after an old girlfriend named Flora, who had a tongue on her like a two-edged sword."

"I thought it was illegal to carry a sword," said Jonathan. "I mean, a dagger."

"In Rome, maybe, but it would be suicide *not* to carry one here in Greece. It's even allowed back there in Corinth." He glanced up at the sky, dark blue and pricked with the first stars of evening. "But even Flora won't help us," he said, "if we're caught around here after dark. We'd better find a place to stay."

"How about that place," said Nubia, pointing toward a two-story building farther up the coast. "That could be a disreputable guesthouse."

They all laughed.

"Don't laugh," said Jonathan, looking up from his guidebook. "I think Nubia's right. This guidebook lists the Diolkos Tavern but doesn't give it even one tower."

SCROLL VII

"Ugh!" said Flavia, as they stepped into their bedroom an hour later. "That was awful: having to eat that gritty porridge with all those men staring at us."

"Only you didn't actually eat any of your gritty porridge," said Jonathan, dropping his knapsack on the large, low bed.

Behind him, Lupus groaned and pinched his nostrils.

"He's right," said Jonathan. "It smells terrible in here!"

"It is most small and dark," said Nubia.

"Oh no!" wailed Flavia, holding up her flickering oil lamp. "There's only one bed!"

"Don't worry, Miss Flavia," said Atticus. "The bed's fairly big. If the four of you lie sideways, you'll all fit on. Tigris and I will curl up here by the door. I'm used to sleeping on my cloak."

"If we lie sideways our feet will hang over the side of the mattress," said Flavia in a small voice.

"Well then," said Jonathan, setting his bow and arrows on the floor, "I'm sure the innkeeper would be happy to chop off our feet at the ankles so we fit." He walked to a dark corner of the room and stared down at a ceramic pot. "No wonder it stinks in here," he said. "I don't think anyone's emptied the vespasian for days. It's full to the brim."

"Ugh!" Flavia shuddered.

"I'll do it," said Atticus. He took a few steps across the room, set his own lamp down on a small table, and elbowed one of the wooden shutters open. Then he carefully lifted the pot and tossed the contents out the window. They heard it splash below and someone shout angrily in Greek.

"Oops!" said Atticus. "Didn't think anyone would be outside after dark!" He set the pot back down in the corner. "Do you girls want to use it first, while we step out in the hall for a moment?"

Flavia nodded and sighed. "Yes, please, Atticus," she reached into her own pack for her sponge stick. "We'll tell you when we've finished." When the bedroom door had shut behind them, she sighed. "Oh, Nubia, I'm so tired. I just know I'll sleep like Hypnos tonight."

Flavia did not sleep like Hypnos.

When the fleas were not biting and the spiders were not dropping onto her face and the sour-smelling straw mattress was not digging into her back, she kept seeing the image of her father's body and her tutor standing wild-eyed over him.

She turned onto her left side and scratched a flea bite. Her father had only ever shown Aristo kindness. Why had he done this terrible thing?

She knew she was ignoring at least one important clue. Maybe more. She cursed silently. She had missed a chance earlier in the day. She should have gone to Aristo's parents' house in Corinth. Helen's slaves had been there looking for him and had found nothing, but she might have discovered something they missed. Maybe he had told his parents something or they had seen him acting strangely.

Flavia rolled onto her back again. Something else wasn't right. Something in the back of her mind half emerged, and she tugged at it as a robin tugs a worm from the soil. Finally she had it. The curse.

Why would one person curse another and then try to kill him? You either cursed someone or killed them, but not both. Yet that was what Aristo must have done, because there was no doubt he was guilty.

Suddenly she heard Tigris growl low in his throat. The door creaked and Flavia lifted her head to see a vertical sliver of light appear in the darkness. Someone was opening the door to their room!

She felt Nubia's hand clutch her own, and she heard Tigris growl again—a deeper, more menacing growl. Then Atticus said something in Greek and kicked the door shut, and the thread of light was extinguished. Silence on the other side of the door. Then footsteps going away.

"Don't worry," came Atticus's deep voice in the darkness. "Whoever he was, he won't be back. Go back to sleep."

Flavia felt relief, then nausea. This was madness. Four children, a big puppy, and an old Greek sailor trying to catch a fugitive in a country they barely knew. What had she been thinking? She should have stayed with her father and used his gold to hire someone to find Aristo.

Then she remembered what Jonathan had said earlier that day. What if all the mysteries she had solved in the past year had been a preparation for this one? If she could work out the motive for the crime, it might help her find Aristo. She would make him tell where he had hidden the lead strip so that they could undo the curse and restore her father's memory. Then her father would be himself again, and they could go home.

She knew she had to find the motive for Aristo's attack on her father, but no solutions came. Only the terrible image of him, lying like a corpse on a bier.

SCROLL VIII

They rose before dawn. In the torchlit stables of the Diolkos Tavern, Nubia helped Atticus harness the mules to the carriage. The mules wore leather chest straps which were attached to the long stick—called a tongue—that pulled the carruca. Helen had named the animals after her four favorite spices: pepper, cumin, coriander, and cinnamon. Piper was the leader and Nubia's favorite. He was dark brown flecked with gray, and very intelligent. Yoked to the wooden tongue next to him was Cuminum, a golden brown mule with long eyelashes and a docile temperament. Coriandrum and Cinnamum were the two following mules. Both were placid and patient. Coriandrum was a slightly lighter brown than Cinnamum, and had a white blaze on his forehead.

Tigris had found Aristo's scent, and soon the mules were trotting briskly after him. The beaten earth road wound along the coast not much above sea level, sometimes rising and sometimes falling. The sun would not rise for nearly an hour, but the sky and sea were already full of a deep vibrant blue light.

They had passed four milestones when the sun pushed up over the horizon to their right, making a molten trail of dazzling light on the sea. Now every rock and blade of grass cast a long shadow, and Nubia felt an immediate delicious warmth where the sunlight touched her. Her stomach growled so she undid one of the nap-kins Helen had prepared for them and passed around pieces of bread spread with soft white cheese.

Tigris had been trotting ahead, nose down, when a large flat rock suddenly took his interest. The carriage rolled past him and Atticus pulled on the reins and they all turned their heads to look back at the big puppy. Tigris gave the flat rock a thorough sniff, then followed his nose across the road and through wildflower-dotted grasses to a nearby olive grove.

"Tigris has found Aristo!" cried Flavia, jumping down from the cart and staring across the road. Her piece of bread and cheese was still in her hand, uneaten. "Hide behind the cart everybody, so he doesn't recognize us."

The sun pulled free of the horizon, and Nubia felt its warmth on her back as she peered over the side of the carruca toward the olive grove. In the pine trees nearby a hundred chaffinches were having a lively discussion, and from somewhere behind them came the soft clank of goat bells. The goats appeared a moment later, swarming around the cart. To Nubia, they smelled exactly like the cheese she had just been eating. She glanced down into the baleful yellow eyes of a she-goat.

Suddenly Tigris appeared from the olive grove on the far side of the road. He was trotting purposefully toward them with some-thing in his mouth.

The goats scattered, jostling each other in their eagerness to get away from the approaching dog. They clanked back the way they had come, and Jonathan stepped from behind the carriage to take the object from Tigris.

"What have you got, boy?" he said, taking a bite of his cheese and bread.

"Snake!" cried Nubia, starting back. "It is a snake!"

"No," said Jonathan through his mouthful, "it's a piece of green cord."

48

"Oh!" said Nubia. "It is part of the curtain rope they used to tie up Aristo."

Lupus nodded vigorously.

"So it is," said Jonathan. "I thought it looked familiar. Good dog." He tossed Tigris his last bite of bread and cheese. The big puppy caught and swallowed it in one gulp, then sat waiting attentively for another.

Flavia took the cord and then dropped it. "Ugh! It's soggy!"

"I think it is being chewed," said Nubia, examining the cord. "Here look like tooth marks . . ."

Lupus suddenly pointed at the goats and then pretended to gnaw something between his two wrists.

Nubia nodded. "Yes! The goats."

"Of course!" cried Jonathan. "Goats will eat almost anything. Aristo must have stretched his arms out behind him and let one of them chew through the cord."

"That was most clever," said Nubia.

"He's probably found himself a pair of sandals by now, too," said Flavia. "So he'll be moving faster."

"But at least this proves we're still on his trail," said Jonathan.

Flavia nodded and tossed her uneaten piece of bread and cheese to Tigris. "Good dog," she said, and to the others, "Let's go. I have a feeling our fugitive is not far off."

"What I don't understand," said Jonathan a short time later, "is why Aristo hit and tried to strangle your father as well as stabbing him."

"Stop it!" cried Flavia, pressing her hands to her ears. "How can you say such a thing when I'm sitting right beside you?"

The carruca was climbing a narrow road along the edge of the cliff. According to Jonathan's guidebook, this part of the road was called the Evil Stairs, and in ancient times it had been the haunt of Sciron, the robber who threw his victims from the precipice into the sea.

"Flavia," said Jonathan. "If you want to find Aristo and solve the mystery of why he attacked your father, then we have to discuss it."

"I know." Flavia sighed. "But it's hard. It's not a random person we're discussing. It's Pater! I feel sick every time I think about it."

"Maybe if we call him something else? Like, the Victim?"

"That makes him sound dead."

"How about the Paterfamilias?"

"Or Marcus?" said Nubia.

Lupus held out his wax tablet. On it he had written:

THE CAPTAIN?

"Those all make me think of Pater," said Flavia.

Lupus scribbled something else, then held up his wax tablet again. On it he had written one word: VIR

Jonathan raised his eyebrows. "That's not bad, Lupus. How about it, Flavia? We'll call him Vir, the Man. Will that work?" he said.

"Maybe," said Flavia, taking a breath. "Let's try."

"OK." Jonathan gripped the edge of the carriage as it rocked, and caught a sickening glimpse over the edge. Far below him on the right, the emerald surface of the sea glittered with a million diamonds of sunlight. Jonathan turned to look at the bone-colored cliffs rearing up on the left. "Let's review the facts," he said. "At dusk on the fourth day of May in a hospitium in the Corinthian port of Cenchrea, a young man named Aristo asked his employer, Vir, if he could be released from a contract two years early."

Flavia nodded. "They decided to discuss it privately. Pater—I mean Vir—doesn't like to talk about money in front of us."

"So they go upstairs to Aristo's room and discuss the breaking of the contract," said Jonathan. "But they disagree, and a heated argument breaks out. Aristo is so angry that he stabs Vir, then bangs his head on the bed, and then tries to strangle him."

"No, no, no," said Flavia. "Yes, they did go to discuss the breaking of the contract at dusk, but the crime didn't occur until three or four hours later, around midnight. It doesn't make sense that Aristo would wait four hours to try to kill . . . Vir."

"It makes sense," said Jonathan, "if Aristo wanted to wait until the victim was asleep and then take him by surprise!"

"Yes," said Flavia slowly. "That might explain something that's been bothering me. Why curse someone if you intend to kill them? But maybe Aristo put the curse on Vir right after their meeting, then later he was afraid it wouldn't work, so then he decided to kill him." She shuddered.

Lupus nodded his agreement but Nubia frowned.

"Why was your father—I mean Vir—in Aristo's bedroom?" she said. "In the Orpheus room."

"Good question," said Jonathan. "It's not very likely that Aristo waited until it was dark and everyone was asleep and then crept into Vir's room and whispered, 'Wake up, sir. I'd like you to come next door so I can attempt to stab, strangle, and beat you.'"

Lupus nodded and pointed at Jonathan, as if to say: He's right.

"And why," said Nubia, "was Vir in Aristo's bed?"

There was a pause, and then Flavia and Jonathan stared at each other wide-eyed.

"You don't think they were . . . ?" said Jonathan.

"No," said Flavia, shaking her head. "Pater only likes women. Aristo, too. I don't think that is the motive."

"I agree," said Nubia, and Lupus nodded, too.

Jonathan scratched his dark, curly hair. "Maybe Aristo laid Vir out on the bed *after* he had stabbed and strangled him!"

"And then covered him with a blanket and stood over him with a bloody knife looking guilty?"

"He did not look guilty," said Nubia suddenly.

51

"What?"

"He looked . . ." Nubia tried to find the word, "he looked horrible. No. I mean *horrified*."

"Yes," said Flavia bitterly. "Horrified by what he had done."

"No," said Nubia, "not by what he had done. Because later he has another thing in his eyes."

"What do you mean?" asked Jonathan and Flavia together, and Lupus gave her his bug-eyed look.

"Pleading," said Nubia. "Yes, that is the word: pleading. There is pleading in his eyes. I do not think that Aristo committed this crime."

"What do you mean: Aristo didn't commit the crime?" asked Flavia angrily. The road was still climbing but it had curved away from the cliff edge, and they were passing through pine woods. "We all saw him standing over the body with a bloody knife in his hand." She shuddered.

"Maybe," said Nubia softly, "Aristo comes upon someone else trying to hurt your . . . Vir. Also, that other person runs away. Remember a person runs by us in the corridor?"

"So Aristo is left standing over the body," said Jonathan. He looked at Flavia. "It's a possibility," he said. "You have to admit that."

"I'll admit it's possible. But if Aristo didn't try to kill Vir, then why didn't he say so? Why didn't he say 'I just saw the person who did it running away!' or something like that? He just let them lead him away like a lamb to the altar. Also, why was he holding the knife? And if he was innocent, why did he run away from the slaves? He could have told the vigiles—ow!" she cried, as Lupus gripped her forearm hard. He had his finger to his lips and his sea-green eyes were open wide in alarm.

"Atticus, stop the carriage!" cried Jonathan.

As Atticus reined in the mules and the cart wheels stopped

grinding, they all heard a scream coming from the sun-dappled woods to their left. Without hesitating, Jonathan reached for his bow and arrows and leaped out of the carruca. In the time it took him to nock an arrow, the others were out, too, running toward the pines. Atticus was in the lead.

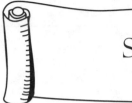

SCROLL IX

As Lupus reached the clearing, he stopped for an instant to take in the scene before him. Atticus was half-crouched, his knife, Flora, flashing in his right hand. Facing him was a rat-faced man whose knife was not much smaller than Flora. A few paces away, by some small boulders, Tigris had seized the ankle of a second man, who was bellowing with pain and trying to hit the growling dog as he hopped on his free foot. Something was crawling in the dust at their feet. It was a boy. A boy in an oversized gray tunic and a grubby blue cloak, his short hair mussed and his face bloody. Robbers and a victim.

Lupus started to untie his belt, which doubled as a sling, but he was suddenly aware of Jonathan beside him, loosing an arrow. The man with the knife screamed as the arrow embedded itself in his upper arm. Then he turned and fled into the woods.

"Let go of him, Tigris!" called Jonathan grimly, pulling another arrow from his quiver. "I don't want you to get hurt when I shoot him, too!"

Tigris instantly released his grip, and Jonathan drew back his bowstring a second time. But the other robber was already crashing off into the bushes after his friend. Jonathan lowered his bow.

"Atticus!" cried Flavia. "Are you all right?"

Atticus was breathing so hard he couldn't speak, but he nodded his head and then pointed toward the boy on the ground.

But Nubia was already there. She had helped the youth to sit up against the rough bark of a pine tree and was giving him a drink from her water gourd. Tigris was sniffing the boy's sandaled feet with interest.

They all stood in a semicircle looking down. The boy was crying. His left cheekbone was red where it had been struck, and his lower lip swollen and bloody. He had pale skin and smooth cheeks, and from this Lupus guessed he was about fourteen or fifteen.

"Are you all right?" said Flavia in Latin.

The boy nodded and winced as Nubia touched her handkerchief to his bloody lip. "Stupid robbers," he said through his tears. "Couldn't they tell I'm just a beggar? I don't even have a copper coin to give them." He spoke good Latin with no trace of an accent.

"You're lucky we came along, young man," said Atticus, who had recovered his breath. "This road isn't one to be traveling on your own. What in Neptune's name is a beggar doing out here anyway? Not much chance of getting alms with only a few mountain goats and a handful of travelers per day."

The boy wiped his nose with his finger. He was trembling. "I'm on my way to Athens," he said, pulling his grubby blue cloak closer around his shoulders. "I thought the pickings might be better there. I've had enough of Corinth."

"What's your name?" Flavia asked the boy.

The boy hesitated, then glanced up at her. "Nikos," he said at last.

"Well, Nikos, we're going toward Athens," said Flavia. "Why don't you come that far with us. We have a carruca," she added.

The boy looked up at them, and Flavia could hear his teeth chattering.

55

"Better make up your mind quickly," said Atticus, glancing around nervously. "I don't want to wait for those robbers to return with their friends!"

"Why are you going to Athens?" said Nikos as he limped after them through the pines to the carruca.

"We're searching for someone." Flavia took a deep breath. "We're searching for the man who tried to kill my father."

Nikos's long-lashed brown eyes opened wider, and his curved dark eyebrows went up.

"A robber tried to kill your father?"

"Not a robber. Our tutor, Aristo."

Nikos stopped. "Not Aristo, son of Diogenes?" he said.

"Yes!" It was Flavia's turn to stop and stare. "How did you know?"

"It's an uncommon name," said Nikos.

"Do you know him?" asked Nubia.

"Of course," said Nikos. "One of my best begging spots is near the well at the end of their street. His family and mine are some of the original Corinthians, pure Greek blood."

"Your family?" asked Jonathan with a frown. "Are they beggars, too?"

"Um . . . no," said Nikos, hanging his head. "They were tragically wiped out by a fever, leaving me a destitute orphan beggar boy."

"Tell us!" cried Flavia, fumbling in her coin purse. "Tell us everything you know about Aristo and his family, and we'll reward you. I'll give you this denarius!"

"I'd rather have your company on the road to Athens," said Nikos, glancing around nervously. He was trembling again. "I want to get there alive."

"You can have both!" cried Flavia, handing him the silver coin. "And if you help us catch Aristo, you can have a gold coin, too!"

■ ■ ■

"Aristo's family was never rich," said Nikos as the carriage began to move. "His father, Diogenes, was a teacher in the agora, until he started to go blind. Even after he lost his sight, he always used to give me a copper when he passed. Sometimes Aristo's mother gave me a piece of bread or fruit on her way to visit a patient. She is a midwife. Dion and Aristo were kind to me, too."

"Who's Dion?" asked Jonathan.

"Dion is Aristo's younger brother," said Nikos.

"He never told us he had a brother," said Flavia. "What's he like?"

"He's a carpenter. He's kind, and helpful, and handsome."

"As handsome as Aristo?" asked Nubia softly.

"They look very similar," said Nikos. "But Dion is taller and more masculine. Sometimes Aristo is almost pretty."

Just like you, thought Flavia, but she did not say the words out loud.

"Do many girls like Aristo?" asked Nubia.

Nikos rolled his brown eyes. "Yes. All the girls like Aristo. Personally, I think Dion would make a far better husband. He's steadier. Less moody. Aristo is so self-obsessed."

"Sounds like you know them very well," said Jonathan.

"When you sit around all day on someone's street, you get to know almost everything about them." As the road curved, Nikos turned his head to stare out over the back of the carriage toward the blue horizon.

"In the past few weeks," said Flavia, "while Aristo has been staying with his parents, have you noticed anything strange about his behavior?"

"Well, he seemed even moodier than usual, if that's possible. Always twanging his lyre."

"Do you not like Aristo's music?" asked Nubia.

"Not really. It's so plinky-plonky and sad and isn't my life miserable."

57

"Aristo is suffering from unrequited love," said Flavia.

"Is he?" Nikos arched an eyebrow. "Serves him right. He's broken enough hearts."

"You don't like him much, do you?" said Flavia, scratching a flea bite on her ankle.

"Frankly, no. Everyone in Corinth seems to think he's Orpheus reborn, especially his parents. Even after he left, he was still their favorite. They were always talking about their wonderful son in Rome who works for a senator."

"He doesn't live in Rome," said Jonathan. "He lives in Ostia, the port of Rome."

"Pater isn't a senator," said Flavia.

"But Aristo is a very good tutor," said Nubia.

Nikos shrugged. "I suppose they exaggerated. All I'm saying is that poor Dion couldn't win."

"Nikos," said Flavia, "can you think of any reason why Aristo would want to murder my father, his employer, who has always been kind to him and was about to take him back to Ostia?"

Nikos slowly shook his head. "I'm sorry," he said. "I don't like Aristo much, but I can't think of any reason he would do such a thing."

"I think the mules are afraid of the cliff," said Nubia to Atticus. "Shall we disembark from the carruca and walk beside them?"

"Good idea," said Atticus, pulling up the carruca. "This road's not getting any wider."

They carefully climbed out the back, led by Tigris, who had been riding with them to rest his paws.

"Look at that!" breathed Flavia. They were at the road's highest point, and the precipitous view over the cliff edge made Nubia catch her breath.

"The sky is so big here," she said. "Also the sea."

"It's very panoramic," said Nikos, the beggar boy.

"What is pamoranic?" asked Nubia.

"Panoramic," corrected Flavia. "It means you can see all around."

Tigris barked and wagged his tail as he sniffed the base of a shrine farther up the road.

"Hark," said Nubia. "Tigris says we are still on Aristo's trail."

"Good," said Flavia. "He can't be far off now, especially as we have transport and he's only on foot."

Jonathan pointed across the bay. "Is Athens over there, Atticus?" He glanced down at his guidebook and then up again. "This is the Saronic Gulf, isn't it?"

Atticus nodded. "Athens is that way all right, though you're looking at Salamis, the famous island where we Athenians conquered the Persian fleet in the greatest sea battle of our history."

"But you can see Athens from here?" asked Flavia.

"Yes. Beyond Salamis. Right on the horizon. It's a little hazy today, but they say that sometimes at sunrise you can see the sunlight spark on the tip of Athena's bronze spear."

"You can see Athena?" said Nubia.

"Athena is the Greek name for Minerva," said Flavia. "The goddess of wisdom and war."

"There's a huge bronze statue of her on the Acropolis," said Atticus. "Her spear is the highest point."

"No," said Jonathan, shading his eyes. "Can't see it."

"Athens," whispered Flavia. "Pater always promised he would take me there one day."

"Behold!" said Nubia. "A strange rock far below. It is all alone in the sea."

"That's probably Sciron's Rock," said Jonathan. "Sciron was the robber I told you about who forced travelers to wash his feet. Then he would kick them over the edge, and his turtle would de-

59

vour them. But Theseus did the same thing to him and that's how he died."

Lupus moved to the cliff edge.

"According to the guidebook," said Jonathan, "Sciron was so evil that after Theseus kicked him over the edge, the sea tossed him back. But the land didn't want his body either so it rejected him, too. Back and forth went Sciron until he ended up suspended between sea and earth. That rock is supposed to be him."

Lupus gave a snort of laughter and took another step forward, so that his toes were hanging over the edge of the shelflike path.

"Lupus, please!" said Atticus. "Come away from the edge!"

Nubia and Atticus moved forward to guide the mules, and presently the carruca reached a little shrine on a narrow strip of shoulder between the road and cliff edge.

"Look!" said Flavia. "This shrine is to Castor and Pollux. It's a sign!"

"Why?" asked Nikos.

"Castor and Pollux are special protectors of my family."

Nubia left Piper and came to look at the shrine. It was made of white marble and shaped like a miniature temple. The brightly painted details had been faded by the sun and wind, but when she bent to look inside she could just make out the twins and their horses painted on the tiny back wall. On the shelf between the two white columns lay offerings left by travelers: bunches of dried wild flowers, a withered apple, a spent candle, and something that looked like a dead snake.

Nubia stretched out a trembling hand and took the piece of green silk cord.

"Eureka!" Flavia snatched it from Nubia and gripped it so hard that her knuckles turned white. "We're still on his trail!" She closed her eyes. "Dear Castor and Pollux," she prayed, "help us catch Aristo and bring him to justice. If you do, I vow to erect an altar to you in Ostia. This is my pledge." She reached around her neck and pulled off a bronze good luck charm that her old nurse-maid, Alma, had given her the month before. Carefully she placed the pendant in the shrine among the other offerings.

Then, drawing back her arm, she threw the piece of curtain cord far out into space. Nubia watched it make a high arc before it fell down and down, onto the jagged rocks far below.

SCROLL X

"Why do you think Aristo is leaving his green cord in the shrine where anybody could see it?" asked Nubia, as the mules began their winding descent. The road had widened, and they were riding in the carruca again.

"No idea," said Jonathan, and Lupus shrugged.

"Megara," said Atticus.

"Yes?" said Nikos, with a look of alarm.

"That's Megara over there," said Atticus. "The town in the middle of that plain."

"Oh," said Nikos. "Of course." He was trembling again, pulling his cloak around him.

"Maybe Aristo wants to give thanks for his escape," said Nubia. "So he leaves green rope in the shrine."

Lupus nodded his agreement.

"Or maybe," said Jonathan, "it was a kind of thanks offering to the gods for setting him free."

"The gods aren't on his side," growled Flavia. "They're on ours."

"Those twin citadels rising behind the town walls are sometimes called the Breasts of Megara," remarked Atticus.

Lupus guffawed.

"Maybe," said Nubia, "Aristo wants us to know where he goes."

Lupus frowned at Nubia and silently mouthed the word Why?

"Of course!" cried Nikos, pointing at Lupus. "You're the boy with no tongue! Aristo often talked about you."

"Good gods!" cried Jonathan. "Did you sit begging under his bedroom window?"

Nikos flushed. "Actually," he said after a moment, "actually, yes. I did sit by their house sometimes."

"And you heard Aristo talking about us?" said Flavia.

"Yes," said Nikos. "I mean . . . well, one time I heard him mention one of his pupils, a little Greek boy who'd seen his father murdered and then had his tongue cut out to stop him from talking. Isn't that a terrible story?"

"Yes, it's terrible," said Jonathan, glancing at Lupus. "Did he ever talk about his other pupils?" he added quickly.

"Yes. There was a Jewish boy who signed up to be a gladiator—Oh! That must be you!"

Jonathan nodded.

"And you must be his master's daughter, bright and bossy."

"Bossy!" growled Flavia. "I'll boss him plenty when I get my hands on him!"

"Did he mention me?" asked Nubia.

"What's your name again?"

"Nubia."

Nikos gathered his blue cloak around his shoulders. "No," he said presently. "I can't remember him ever mentioning an African girl or anyone named Nubia."

"Oh," said Nubia, and hung her head.

"Here, Lupus," said Atticus, "you can take the reins now that the road's leveling out."

"You're in love with him!" cried Nikos suddenly.

"Of course I'm not," said Atticus, ruffling Lupus's hair. "I just think he's special. Last month on the ship during a storm there was a light glowing around his head, and that means he's favored by the gods."

They all stared at the gray-haired Greek.

"I wasn't talking to you," said Nikos. "I was talking to Nubia. You're in love with Aristo, aren't you?"

Nubia covered her face with her hands.

"Of course she's not!" cried Flavia, putting a protective arm around her friend. "We saved your life, and all you can do is call me bossy and accuse Nubia of loving a murderer."

"Sorry!" said Nikos. He turned his head to look toward the twin mounds on which the town was built. "I'm just trying to help you catch the fugitive."

"Um . . . according to my guidebook," said Jonathan quickly, "there's a famous well in Megara. It's um . . . called the Fountain of Theagenes. They say the water of the nymphs flows into it. Its roof stands on a hundred columns made of soft white stone full of seashells."

"That's true," said Atticus. "I've seen it."

"Flavia," said Jonathan, "back in Ostia, whenever your cook, Alma, wants to hear the latest news, she always goes to the public fountain, doesn't she?"

Flavia nodded. "The fountain is where all the women go to gossip." Her gray eyes widened. "We could go there now!" she said. "It's almost noon and it probably won't be very crowded, but still . . . someone might have seen Aristo. Atticus, do you remember where the fountain is?'

"Of course," said Atticus with a chuckle. "It's in the cleavage between the breasts of Megara."

"So this is the famous Fountain of Theagenes," said Flavia.

"It resembles more a temple than fountain." Nubia tipped her head back to look at the lofty red-tiled roof. "Behold!" she said. "The women carry jars on their head like in my country."

Lupus grunted and brought his nose close to one of the white columns.

"It does have little shells in it," said Nikos. "Tiny sparkly shells."

"No, Tigris!" cried Jonathan. "Not at the base of the column! Do it by a tree and then wait with Atticus by the carruca."

Flavia led the way through the columns into a shady, cool space full of the echoing sound of running water and women's chatter. Although it was noon, there were more than twenty women there. At both ends marble lions spouted water into long troughs, into which the women dipped their water jars. As the women saw the strangers, they grew quiet and some of them covered their heads or faces with their mantles.

Flavia stepped forward and in a clear voice she recited the Greek phrase she had been practicing: "Good day, women of Megara. We are looking for this man. Do you know him?"

Lupus stepped forward and held up the picture he had painted on the wax tablet. Then he slowly revolved, so they could all see the portrait.

A few women shyly moved forward and began to whisper excitedly to each other as they studied the image. Nikos leaned forward with interest, too, and when he saw the portrait he raised his eyebrows in surprise. Other women came up to look, and once again the space beneath the roofed fountain was full of echoing chatter.

"What are they saying?" Flavia asked Lupus. "Do they recognize him?"

He nodded his head, and two slender young women pushed forward.

"My friend and I," said one of the women in Latin, "we see this man on the road to Athens at daybreak." The woman was pretty despite a strawberry-colored birthmark on her cheek. "He frightens us because he has dried blood on his tunic."

"And because he is saying crazy things," said her brown-eyed friend.

"He told you crazy things?" asked Flavia.

"Not to us. No. He is speaking with himself," said the girl with the birthmark.

The brown-eyed girl nodded vigorously. "He is saying in Greek, 'Go away, leave me alone!' He is sometimes running and sometimes walking and sometimes looking behind him."

The first girl interrupted. "He says they are after him and he keeps saying, 'Forgive me! I'm sorry! I didn't mean to do it!' and he brushes at his clothings as if flies are crawling on him."

"He keeps speaking of the Kindly Ones," said the brown-eyed girl. "He is crazy."

"But he is handsome," added her friend, and they began to giggle.

"I saw him, too," said a quiet voice, "and I think my friends are mistaken."

Flavia turned to see an older woman with eyes as black as her garments. Her face was lined but still beautiful.

The woman touched Aristo's portrait with her forefinger. "I saw this man on the road to Athens. I was milking my goats in a field by the side of the road. He was striding down the road, and his red mantle caught my eye. When he saw me looking at him, he stopped and asked me for a drink of goat's milk. I gave him one. He looked tired and pale but he was very polite and quite sane. He said he could not pay me for the goat's milk, but he asked the gods to reward me. He was certainly not crazy."

"When was this?"

"An hour or two after dawn."

"Did he have blood on his tunic?"

"I couldn't tell. He wore a red cloak over it."

Flavia turned to the two younger women. "But the man you saw definitely had a bloodstained tunic."

The brown-eyed woman nodded. "My husband is a butcher. I

66

know very well what dried blood looks like. It was a white tunic with dried blood here and here." She pointed to her chest and thighs. "We did not see that he was wearing a cloak."

Flavia grasped Lupus's wrist and made him hold up the tablet again. "You're absolutely positive this is the man?"

All three of them nodded.

SCROLL XI

On the road from Megara to Eleusis they stopped to speak to a farmer in his vineyard, an imperial messenger on horseback, and the driver of an oxcart transporting a large cube of Pentilic marble. The farmer identified the man in Lupus's portrait as tired but polite when he asked for food. But the messenger and cart driver had seen the man painted on Lupus's tablet jogging and babbling to himself. "Ran straight for my oxen," the cart driver had said. "Almost got himself trampled into the dust." None of the three remembered seeing a red cloak.

"If only we could catch him before he gets to Eleusis," said Flavia, as the carruca rattled on through the bright morning. "This mystery seems to get more confusing every time we meet someone. First we hear that Aristo is mad and raving, the next he's politely asking for food. It's almost as if there were two Aristos."

"Now what?" said Jonathan. He stood at a fork in the road with his hands on his hips looking up at an inscribed column of marble. The red-painted letters in the white marble milestone told him that the road on the right led to Eleusis and Athens, while the road on the left would take them to Thebes and Delphi. Tigris was sniffing among the wildflower-dotted grasses by the side of the Athens Road.

"Which way do we go?" said Jonathan. "Athens or Thebes?" He absently kicked a pile of cinnamon-colored feathers at the side of the road, where some animal had caught a turtledove.

"I don't know," said Flavia, staring around in frustration. "I don't understand why we haven't caught him by now."

"Maybe he got a lift or stole a horse," said Jonathan.

"Unless he heard our carriage coming and hid in the bushes," said Flavia. "Which means he knows we're after him."

"Where do you think he was headed, Miss Flavia?" asked Atticus. "Any idea?"

"I thought you said he was going to Athens," said Nikos.

"No," said Flavia. "We said he'd been seen on the Athens Road. That doesn't necessarily mean he's going there, though he probably is," she added.

"Why?" said Jonathan. "Why would he go to Athens?"

"To get a fast ship away from Greece?" said Flavia.

"There are far more ships sailing from Cenchrea and Lechaeum," said Atticus. "You Romans always forget that Athens is just a small academic town these days. Corinth is much bigger and richer, and it has ten times as much sea traffic."

"I suppose there's no reason for him to go to Thebes or Delphi," said Jonathan, looking at the milestone.

"Wait!" cried Flavia. "Yes, there is! Of course! Why didn't I think of it sooner?"

"What?" they all cried.

"Remember the women at the fountain in Megara? One of them said he was ranting about the Kindly Ones?"

"Does that mean something?" said Jonathan. "It sounded like gibberish to me."

"The Kindly Ones. How do you say that in Greek, Atticus?"

But Nikos answered first. "*Eumenides,*" he said.

Atticus nodded and said in a harsh whisper, "The Ones Who Must Not Be Named!" He spat and made the sign against evil.

"What?" said Jonathan. "What are you all babbling about?"

"Orestes," said Flavia. "Remember the story of Orestes, the son of Agamemnon?"

"Wasn't he the one who killed his own mother?" said Jonathan.

"He kills his own mother?" gasped Nubia.

"Yes," said Atticus, "because she killed his father."

"That's right," said Flavia. "Clytemnestra murdered her husband, Agamemnon, the night he returned from Troy."

"But Clytemnestra only killed Agamemnon because he killed their oldest daughter, Iphigenia," said Nikos. "Agamemnon sacrificed their daughter to bring favorable winds, so the fleet could sail to Troy."

Nubia frowned. "So the father kills the daughter and then the mother kills the father for revenge and then the son kills the mother for more revenge?"

Flavia nodded. "Terrible, isn't it? Poor Orestes didn't even want to kill his mother, but the god Apollo told him to do it."

"Although he did it at Apollo's command," said Atticus, "the deed brought down the wrath of the Kindly Ones, who pursue the guilty."

"I still do not understand who these Kindly Ones are," said Nubia.

Flavia whispered something in her ear.

"The Furies?" said Nubia.

"Shhh!" they all cried. Flavia, Nikos, and Atticus all made the sign against evil.

"I told you," hissed Atticus, glancing around nervously, "they are the Ones Who Must Not Be Named! They're terrible creatures who look like women but have snaky hair."

"Like Medusa," said Nubia, "who is making men stone with one look?"

"Exactly," said Flavia, "only they don't turn you to stone. They drive you slowly insane. They don't just have snaky hair but they also have snakes coiling around their arms and slithering all over their bodies. They have red eyes and dripping fangs and black tongues and long sharp fingernails. They crack whips and carry torches because they always come in the night." She made the sign against evil.

"I do not like people with snakes slithering over their bodies," said Nubia in a small voice.

"But what do the . . . the Kindly Ones have to do with Thebes?" asked Jonathan.

"Not Thebes," said Flavia. "Delphi. They pursued Orestes after his crime, and no matter where he went he couldn't escape them. Finally he journeyed to Delphi to seek sanctuary."

"What is seek sanctuary?" asked Nubia.

"If you commit a crime," said Flavia, "especially murder, and you go to a temple and cling to the god's altar then nobody can harm you. You're safe until the priests purify you."

"Why did Orestes go all the way to Delphi?" asked Jonathan. "Weren't there any altars where he lived?"

"I think it's because Delphi is where Apollo's special sanctuary is located. So he went there to ask Apollo how he could be set free from the Kindly Ones."

"Did it work?"

"I can't remember exactly," said Flavia. "I was sick on Pater's tunic."

They all stared at her.

"He took me to see the play," she explained. "But I was only seven and I ate too many currants and when the Kindly Ones appeared onstage I was so terrified that I threw up in Pater's lap. So we had to leave the theater, and I don't know what happened after that. That's why I don't like currants," she added. "Or raisins."

"So you think Aristo is being hounded by the Kindly Ones because of his guilt," said Jonathan, "and that he's gone to Delphi to ask Apollo how to stop them from tormenting him?"

Flavia nodded. "Just like Orestes."

"I think you are right," said Nubia quietly. "I think Aristo has gone to Delphi."

"You sound very certain," said Nikos.

"It is not me who is certain," said Nubia, "but Tigris."

She pointed to a pomegranate tree about twenty paces along the left-hand fork of the road. The big puppy's nose was buried in the wildflowers at the base of its trunk, and his tail was a blur of excitement.

SCROLL XII

Lupus crouched beside Tigris and examined the grasses at the base of the pomegranate tree. After a few moments he stood up and shook his head.

"No trace of anything?" said Atticus. "Are you sure it's Aristo he smells, and not a rabbit or a weasel?"

"Tigris knows who we're looking for," said Jonathan, and gazed thoughtfully back toward the main road, where the carriage stood beneath some pine trees. The four mules dozed in the shade.

"I think I can guess what happened," he said. "Aristo probably got a cart driver to give him a lift, or hitched a ride on the back of one, but it was going to Athens rather than Delphi so he jumped off there at the crossroads. He started along this road and probably stopped to make water here."

Lupus nodded. That made sense.

"Let's carry on, then," said Atticus. "We can't be far behind him now."

"Good!" said Flavia, and turned to Nikos. "Well, I guess we have to say good-bye here; you'll want the road to Athens."

Nikos stared at them with his long-lashed brown eyes.

"Aren't you going to Athens?" asked Flavia. "You said the pickings might be better there."

Nikos looked at the Athens Road, then back at them. "If you

don't mind," he said, "I . . . I'd like to come with you to Delphi. I've never seen it and you've all been so kind to me. I'll help you find Aristo," he added quickly.

When Lupus saw that Flavia was about to agree, he flashed her a quick warning frown.

"Um . . . let me just say something to Lupus," said Flavia. She took Lupus a few steps farther up the road. "What is it, Lupus?" she said in a low voice. "Don't you want Nikos to come with us? He speaks Greek and could be very useful. Also, he knows what Aristo looks like."

Lupus wrote on his wax tablet:

SOMETHING NOT RIGHT ABOUT HIM

"What?"
Lupus shrugged, then scowled, then shrugged again.

From the milestone Jonathan called out, "Flavia! You have to hear this!"

"What?" she called out.

"Nikos thinks he's solved the mystery!"

"What mystery?"

"The mystery of the two Aristos!"

"Tell us how there can be two Aristos!" said Flavia to Nikos. They had moved to stand by the mules in the shade of the pines. Atticus and Nubia were feeding the mules with bags full of beans mixed with wine-soaked barley.

Nikos lowered his voice. "Two Aristos, one of them sane, and the other one mad."

"Yes, yes. Tell us!"

"Lupus, show me your wax tablet," said Nikos.

Lupus passed him the tablet.

Nikos tapped the portrait. "This is Aristo, correct?"

"Yes," said Flavia. "You should know that. You said you've sat begging near his house."

"But it doesn't look *exactly* like Aristo."

"Well of course not. It's a painting. It's a likeness. But you can easily see it's Aristo, can't you?"

"Of course," said Nikos. "But it could also be Dion."

"Dion?" said Flavia with a frown.

"Aristo's younger brother," said Nubia over her shoulder.

"I don't understand," said Flavia.

"When Lupus showed this portrait at the well, I thought it was Dion, not Aristo."

"Oh," said Flavia, and then as understanding dawned: "*Oh! We're not the only ones pursuing Aristo!*"

Nikos nodded.

"Dion's after him, too," said Jonathan. "He must have heard about what Aristo did."

Flavia nodded. "Helen's slaves went to Aristo's house to search for him there. That's probably when his brother found out what happened."

"That explains," said Nikos, "why some people see Aristo, bloody and pursued by demons, and others see Dion—who looks very like Aristo—in close pursuit."

"That's brilliant, Nikos!" said Flavia. "Why didn't I think of that?"

"Because you've never seen Dion, but I have. I know what he looks like."

"He looks that much like Aristo?" said Jonathan.

Nikos nodded.

"Are they twins?" asked Flavia.

"No, Aristo is three years older. But they look very alike."

WHY DIDN'T YOU TELL US BEFORE, wrote Lupus. THAT DION IS ALSO AFTER ARISTO?

"I only just realized." Nikos bent to pluck a stalk of grass from the roadside.

"But why is the Dion pursuing Aristo?" said Nubia.

"Here in Greece," said Nikos, "the crime of murder—or even attempted murder—brings disgrace on a family. Unless it's for revenge. If Dion catches Aristo and brings him to justice, then his family's honor will be restored."

"Or maybe Dion wants to help Aristo escape!" cried Flavia.

"I don't think so," said Nikos. "They don't like each other. In fact, they hate each other."

"What will Dion do to Aristo if he catches him?" asked Nubia, lowering the feed bag from Cuminum's nose.

"The same thing you intend to do, I imagine." Nikos looked at Flavia. "Take him back to Corinth and make him stand trial. Of course your father would have to bring suit, because he is the injured party."

"But what if Pater's not well enough?" asked Flavia. "What if he still can't remember who he is?"

"If nobody calls Aristo to trial," said Nikos, "then he goes free. Achaea is a province of Rome, so its laws are the same."

Flavia suddenly narrowed her eyes at Nikos. "Wait. How do you know so much about Roman law?"

"Lawyers can be pompous snobs," said Nikos, nibbling his stalk of grass, "but when they win a case they are extremely generous. I often sit in the colonnade of the basilica on days of public trials."

"Well, if you know what Dion looks like then I think you should definitely come with us to Delphi. Are we all agreed?" Flavia glanced at Lupus.

Lupus sighed and nodded. He wasn't sure why he didn't trust Nikos. But all his instincts told him something wasn't right.

It was midafternoon by the time they had found a stream to water the mules and set off inland on the road to Thebes.

Fed and watered, the mules attacked the mountain road with renewed vigor. By the time the sun began to set over a glittering bay far to the west, they had passed two ancient forts and crossed three pine-clad ridges. But they had not seen a trace of either Aristo or Dion.

At the summit of the last pass, Atticus tugged the mules to a stop, and as the grinding of the wheels ceased, Flavia's world was suddenly filled with silence. She could only hear the sound of the mules breathing, and the wind in the treetops and lazy birdsong. The pine-covered slopes rolled down to a great flat plain below them, with the gleaming mirrors of two lakes beyond and distant mountains on the horizon.

"That's Boeotia," said Atticus, and chuckled. "Cow land. Its capital, Thebes, is down there. The town of Oedipus. You can't see it. It's hidden by that hill. Over there on the left is the plain of Plataea, where we Greeks finally defeated the Persian army. And can you see those two snowcapped peaks far off on the western horizon, silhouetted by the setting sun? Those are Helicon and Parnassus. Delphi," he added.

The others shaded their eyes against the sun and looked toward the horizon, but Flavia kept her eyes on the road ribboning down before them. At this point it was no more than a dirt track with wheel ruts carved in it by a hundred carts.

"No sign of him," she said. "No sign of anyone. We should have caught him by now."

"Um, Flavia?" said Jonathan. "What exactly will we do when we catch him?"

"Tie him up and throw him in this carruca and take him back to Corinth," said Flavia grimly.

"What if he resists?"

"Shoot him with your bow and arrow."

Suddenly Jonathan turned his head and looked toward the pine woods on their left. "Shhh!" he hissed. "Nobody move." He slowly

77

leaned forward and took his bow from the floor of the carruca underneath the bench. Nikos and Atticus had twisted around on the seat at the front, and they all stared wide-eyed as Jonathan extracted an arrow from the quiver and nocked it. Slowly he sat up, took careful aim into the woods, and loosed his arrow.

"Venison smells delicious," said Nubia an hour later.

Lupus nodded his agreement.

"It needs a little longer," said Jonathan. "It's not quite done."

Jonathan's small deer had been drinking at a freshwater spring overhung by a fig tree and surrounded by maidenhair ferns. They had pulled up the carriage under the shelter of some nearby pines, and Nubia had carried a wooden bucket back and forth from the spring to water the mules. Lupus had made a fire while Jonathan and Atticus hung and skinned the deer. They had cut up the best parts into cubes, which Flavia and Nikos had skewered onto twigs sharpened by Lupus. Tigris was given his pick of the rest.

Now they were sitting around the fire, cooking the meat.

"That mountain," said Atticus, pointing with his skewer, "is famous. It's Mount Cithaeron, where Oedipus's parents exposed him after the prophecy."

"What is exposed?" asked Nubia.

"It's when you abandon a baby on a mountain or beside a river," said Atticus. "That way it's not murder, because the gods can always save the baby."

"Why did they abandon their tiny baby?" said Nubia.

Atticus nodded. "Because of the prophecy, that the baby would grow up to kill his father and marry his mother."

"Oh!" cried Nubia, and nearly dropped her skewer in the fire.

"Exposing baby Oedipus didn't do any good, did it?" said Nikos.

"No," said Jonathan. "You can never escape a prophecy."

"Oedipus grew up in Corinth, didn't he?" said Flavia.

"Yes," said Atticus. "A shepherd found the baby and took him to Corinth, where the king and queen longed for a child of their own. They loved him and raised him, but when he was older he began to suspect they weren't his real parents."

"So he got a prophecy, too," said Jonathan.

"Yes. He went to Delphi and asked the oracle if the King and Queen of Corinth were really his parents."

"But the Pythia didn't answer his question," said Flavia. "Instead, she warned him that he would murder his father and marry his mother. Oedipus was horrified, so instead of returning to Corinth he headed away from it."

"But by trying to escape the prophecy," said Jonathan, "he made it come true."

"What is Pythia?" asked Nubia.

"The Pythia is a priestess of Apollo whom the god speaks through," said Flavia. "She's like the Sibyl in Italia."

Jonathan took his skewer away from the flames and blew on the meat. "Don't they say that if you have a problem nobody else can solve, the Pythia will find the answer?"

"That's right," said Flavia.

Jonathan nibbled at the cube of venison on the end of his skewer. "It's ready," he said.

"It's wonderful," said Atticus, a few moments later.

"The best thing I've ever tasted," said Nikos.

"Don't you like yours, Flavia?" asked Jonathan.

"I'm sorry, Jonathan. Every time I try to eat something I feel sick. Atticus," she said, "will we reach Delphi tomorrow?"

"I doubt it," said Atticus. "It's probably fifty miles from here."

"Then can we keep going tonight?"

"What? After dark?"

"Yes, please," said Flavia. "We've got to catch him soon."

Atticus sucked his breath through his teeth. "I don't know,

Miss Flavia," he said. "There's no moon tonight. It will be very dark."

"Helen said we could take off the awning and put torches in the holes on each corner of the carruca to light our way. There are four new ones under one of the benches."

"I suppose we could do that," said Atticus, scratching the base of his woolly gray ponytail. "The road down the mountain isn't a proper road, just wheel ruts. On rut roads like these if you meet a cart coming the other way there's always an awful battle about who should go back. If we travel at night there'll be less chance of us meeting someone."

"See?" said Flavia. "It was a good idea."

"Very well, Miss Flavia. You're the boss. Night travel it is." He wiped his mouth on his sleeve and stood up. "Miss Nubia," he said, "will you help me hitch these mules to their carriage again?"

As the carruca rolled down toward the dark plain, Nubia tipped her head back and looked up at the stars blazing in the sky above her. She could see them clearly despite the circle of light thrown by the torches set in each corner of the carruca.

Flavia pointed. "Look, Nubia, those two bright stars are the Twins, the Gemini. Oh please, Castor and Pollux," she whispered, "protect us on our journey and help us find the culprit."

Nikos wrapped his cloak around his slender body and stretched out on one of the padded benches. "I'm going to sleep," he said.

"Good idea," said Atticus over his shoulder. "Why don't you all try to get some sleep? I'll wake you if I see anyone," he added.

"May I come under your cloak, Nubia?" asked Flavia.

Nubia nodded, and they squeezed together on their padded bench.

"I'll sleep here on the floor," said Jonathan. "Lupus, you can share the other bench with Nikos."

Lupus was sitting at the front beside Atticus. He turned around and shook his head and pointed down as if to say, "I'm staying here."

"Suit yourself," said Jonathan and stretched out on the floor beside Tigris.

"Will you be all right down there on those hard boards?" asked Flavia.

"Yes," said Jonathan. "The Spartans used to sleep on wooden benches with no padding and only a thin blanket in winter. I'll be fine."

Nikos snorted from his padded bench, but presently they were quiet and the only sound Nubia could hear was the constant dull rumble of the carriage and the mules' hooves. The spring night was mild, but Nubia was glad of the double cloaks and Flavia's warm body beside her.

"The stars console you, don't they, Nubia?" whispered Flavia.

"Yes," said Nubia softly. "They console me. They remind me of times my family would all sleep out under the stars in the desert. Before the slave traders come."

"Do you have constellations?"

"Yes, we have star groups, but they are different from yours."

"Show me."

"Well," said Nubia, pointing, "that is the big camel. That is the middle camel, and that is the little camel."

"Don't you have any constellations that aren't camels?"

Nubia smiled. "Yes," she said, "we have twelve that wheel in the sky. . . . The leopard, the jackal, the hyena, the cobra, the scorpion—"

"Oh! We have the scorpion, too. I wonder if it's the same group of stars . . ."

"Yes, it is the same."

"How do you know that?"

"Aristo told me one time."

"When?"

"On board the *Delphina* last month before we reach Corinth. He shows me some star groups and he tells me about the scorpion who rises before the Saturnalia."

"Nubia . . ."

"Yes?"

"Remember that dance we did after the Saturnalia last year . . . to cure love's passion?"

"Yes."

"Did it work? For you, I mean. Did it cure your passion?"

"At first I thought yes. But then I realize that I still love him."

"Aristo. You still love Aristo."

"Yes."

"Even after what he did to Pater?"

"I do not believe Aristo did this thing."

"That's right," said Flavia coldly, rolling over so that her back was to Nubia. "I forgot about that. Good night."

"Good night, Flavia," said Nubia quietly. "I wish you good dreams."

They reached Thebes at dawn and stopped for breakfast at a two-tower hospitium beside the town walls.

A yawning slave boy brought them unglazed bowls of porridge and hot spiced wine.

"Did anyone hear that strange sound last night?" asked Jonathan, taking a sip from his beaker.

"What kind of strange sound?" said Flavia.

"It sounded like evil laughter."

They all looked at each other, then shook their heads.

"But carruca is deep rumbly," said Nubia. "It is hard to hear something when it is moving."

"Then nobody heard it?"

Lupus shook his head.

Jonathan sighed. "Porridge, again," he said, eating a spoonful. "I think this one has some kind of animal fat in it."

"You know what they say about food in Greece," said Atticus cheerfully. 'Porridge, and then more porridge.'"

"The cinnamon on top is nice," said Nubia.

Jonathan stretched and yawned. "Oh, I'd give anything for an hour at the baths," he said.

Lupus nodded his agreement.

"There's a new public bathhouse just inside the Electra Gate," said the serving boy, as he took up the empty bowls. "But it's women only in the mornings."

Flavia turned to Nubia. "Shall we go for a hot bath?"

"Oh, yes, please!" cried Nubia.

"Any men's baths nearby?" asked Jonathan.

"We have a small hot plunge here," said the boy. "No steam room or frigidarium, though."

"I don't mind," said Jonathan. "All I want is to wash off the dust and have a good soak."

"Why don't you all visit the baths, then?" said Atticus. "I'll go ask the authorities if they've seen any bloodstained fugitives."

"Oh, thank you, Atticus," said Flavia. "An hour is all we need."

"Should be enough time for me to find out," said Atticus. He shouldered his leather knapsack and left the courtyard.

Jonathan stood up. "A hot bath will be so good right now. Coming, Lupus? Nikos?"

Lupus jumped up from the table, but Nikos shook his head. "No, thanks."

"Don't worry about the cost," said Flavia. "I'll pay."

"Thanks, but no."

"Are you certain?" said Jonathan. "I don't mean to be rude, but you smell like a mule."

"I'm certain." Nikos pulled his cloak around him like a protective shell.

Jonathan put up both hands, palms out. "Suit yourself," he said, and went off with Lupus.

83

Under the table, Tigris whined.

"Oh no," said Flavia. "What are we going to do with you? We should have sent you with Atticus."

"I can stay with Tigris in the carriage." Nikos yawned, showing even, white teeth. "I didn't sleep very well last night. I'm still tired."

"Oh, thank you, Nikos," said Flavia. "Come on, Nubia. I'm desperate for a good hot soak."

Flavia was fuming. "Where is Atticus?" she cried. "We've been back from the baths for nearly two hours. We could be halfway to Delphi by now!"

"Or at least halfway to The Split," said Jonathan, his head bent over his guidebook. "That's the famous crossroads where Oedipus killed his father."

"Jonathan, will you put that silly book away! You're not helping!"

"I'm sorry, but I thought I *was* helping," said Jonathan coldly. "That's why I've been rattling around in this carriage inhaling dust and fumes from mules' backsides and swatting away their flies."

"Please do not argue," said Nubia. "Look! Here comes Atticus now, looking most worried."

"So he should," growled Flavia, and to Atticus, "Where have you been?"

"I'm sorry, Miss Flavia," said Atticus. "I went to ask the authorities if they'd seen your fugitive. Or his brother. They made me wait and I must have dozed off. It turned out to be a wasted trip, they haven't seen anything."

"Oh, Atticus, I'm sorry," said Flavia. "I forgot you were awake all night. Why don't you sleep now? Nubia can drive. Or Lupus. The road is flat," she added.

"I would love a little nap," he said. "I think Nubia can handle the team. But only as far as the mountains, mind. Then the road gets tricky, as I recall."

As the road began to climb up through a landscape of pines and gray stony hills, Nubia glanced over her shoulder at Atticus, who was snoring gently on his pile of blankets on the floor of the carruca. Lupus grinned; he was sitting beside her at the front.

"Shall we wake him?" Nubia asked Flavia. "As he requested?"

"These are hardly the mountains, yet," said Flavia. "Let him sleep a little longer. If you're still happy driving, that is."

"I am most happy driving," said Nubia. She gazed at the puffy white clouds blanketing the tops of the mountain range ahead, and wondered if the road would take them up that high. She had never been inside a cloud before.

Jonathan glanced up from his guidebook. "This is interesting," he said. "A thousand years ago a young goatherd wandered into the cleft of Delphi with his flock. He smelled a wonderful sweet smell and started to prophesy. That was when people first realized there was something special about Delphi. Some of the old gods occupied it first, but then Apollo decided he wanted it. Oh, you'll like this, Nubia. There's a huge snake in this story."

"Of all creatures I do not like the snake," said Nubia, without turning around. They had left the ruts behind, and she needed to concentrate on guiding the mules along the bumpy road of hard-packed earth.

"Well," said Jonathan. "You certainly would not have liked *this* snake. It was called Python and it lived in a cave at Delphi. Apollo killed it when he took the sanctuary for his own, and the priestess who gives the oracle is called the Pythia after it."

"Is she having snaky hair like Medusa or the Kindly Ones?" asked Nubia.

"No," said Jonathan. "According to this, she's just a priestess who's been specially trained to give the oracle."

85

"What is oracle?"

"Sometimes when people want important advice or need help," said Flavia, "they ask the gods. Like Orestes when he wanted to know how to stop the Kindly Ones from pursuing him. Or Oedipus when he wanted to know if the King and Queen of Corinth were really his parents."

Jonathan turned a papyrus page. "This says the word 'oracle' can refer to the person who gives it, the place it's given, or the prophecy itself."

"But oracle did not help Oedipus," said Nubia, keeping her eyes on the road. It was climbing more steeply now.

"That's right," said Jonathan. "It says here that the Pythia's answers can be ambiguous."

"What is ambiguous?" asked Nubia without turning around.

"Oh, I know!" said Flavia. "It's when something can mean one of two things but it's not clear which. Like when Xerxes asked the Pythia if he should attack another country and she said if he attacked, then a great kingdom would be destroyed and so he attacked and was defeated because—you see—it was his own kingdom that was destroyed."

"It wasn't Xerxes," said Jonathan.

"Yes it was," said Flavia. "I'm sure it was Xerxes."

"No, it wasn't," said Jonathan. "It was a king of Lydia named Croesus. It's right here in the book: 'Before Croesus sought advice about his invasion of Persia, he wanted to test the oracles. So he sent envoys to all the famous ones. On a certain day that had been agreed beforehand, each of the envoys went to a different oracle and asked what Croesus was doing on that day.'"

"And?" said Flavia.

"Only two got it right and the Pythia was one: 'King Croesus,' she said, 'is cooking tortoise and lamb in a bronze cauldron.'"

"That's what he was doing?" asked Flavia, her gray eyes wide.

Jonathan nodded.

Flavia shivered. "Amazing."

Jonathan snorted. "But then—when he finally asks his really important question—about going to war—she gives him that ambiguous message."

Next to Nubia at the front, Lupus shook his head and looked up at the heavens, as if to say: Strange.

"'But despite her ambiguous answers,'" read Jonathan, "'people still flock to ask her questions, and on the seventh day of every month you will find a long line outside the Temple of Apollo.'"

"Today's the seventh day of the month," murmured Flavia. "Or is it the sixth?"

Lupus suddenly turned to look at Jonathan and Flavia.

"What is it, Lupus?" said Jonathan.

Lupus pulled out his wax tablet and wrote on it and showed it to them.

"Of course there's a temple of Apollo at Delphi," said Flavia. "Delphi is Apollo's main sanctuary."

"That's right," said Jonathan, "it's the center of Apollo's cult. The center of the world, in fact. Did you know you can see the navel of the world at Delphi? It's called the omphalos."

"Why do you ask, Lupus?" said Flavia. "Do you think it's a clue?"

But before Lupus could reply, the carruca suddenly shuddered and swung to the left. Nubia felt something in the harness give way, and now the mules were going forward and the carruca was slowing down. The reins were suddenly taut in her hands, and she knew that somehow the harness had come loose. As she felt herself being pulled off her seat she dropped the reins and commanded Piper to stop. He tossed his head and snorted and came to a halt, but now it was too late. Completely free of the mules, the carruca had begun to roll backwards, and on the steep slope it was gathering speed. Nubia heard screams behind her—Flavia and Nikos—and when she looked back, she understood why.

The carruca was rolling straight for a precipice.

SCROLL XIII

Jonathan thought quickly.

There was no mechanism to stop the carriage. Without the mules to make it speed up or slow down, it was just a wood and wicker box on wheels. Wheels! How could he lock the wheels? He had to wedge them with something. He quickly knelt beside Atticus, still snoring among his blankets, and looked under the bench, where they kept the awning and other equipment. He pulled out one of the pine torches they had used the night before. It was as thick as his forearm and about a yard long.

"Hang on!" he shouted. Gripping the torch with both hands, he pulled his arms back, then drove it forward through the wicker side of the carruca.

Instantly one of the spokes caught it and jammed it against a timber in the side. The wheel stopped, and the carruca swung violently around the pivot of the stationary wheel, scattering gravel and dust. Nubia cried out as she was almost thrown from her ledge at the front.

"Lupus!" shouted Jonathan, hanging on to the end of his torch, "Do your side!" He could sense his torch beginning to splinter. If it broke, they would start rolling again, right over the edge. Lupus used a second torch to spear his side of the carriage, and at last the carruca stopped straining toward the drop.

In the silence that followed, they could hear a raven cawing and the sound of something crashing down the mountainside. Jonathan peered over Nubia's trembling shoulder and saw a boulder leaping down and down, getting smaller and smaller. They were only inches from the edge of the precipice.

"What on earth?" Atticus sat up, disheveled and blinking in the back of the carruca. "What happened?"

"We almost went over the cliff," whispered Flavia, "but Jonathan saved us."

"Out!" cried Atticus. "Everybody out of the carriage, for Neptune's sake! I told you to wake me when we reached the mountains."

"We were talking," said Flavia, "and we didn't notice."

"And harness comes loose," said Nubia.

They all piled out of the carruca, and Jonathan had to hold on to its side for a moment until his knees stopped shaking.

While Nubia went to get the mules, the rest of them carefully removed the torches from the spokes, and with the help of Atticus they pulled the carruca to a level place on the safe side of the road. Nubia was speaking softly to the mules and leading them back. They still wore their leather chest straps, but the harness trailed in the dirt behind them. Jonathan took one of the leather straps and examined it.

"It's been cut," he called to Atticus. "So has this one. This was no accident. Somebody cut every strap of the harness."

Atticus joined Jonathan and nodded grimly as he fingered the leather. "You're right," he said. "These have been deliberately cut, and so have the straps attaching them to the wooden tongue. Someone's trying to stop us."

"Aristo!" said Flavia. "Aristo must have done it this morning when we were having breakfast in Thebes. He knew we were getting too close."

"Can you repair the harness?" asked Jonathan.

"We could have been killed!" said Flavia.

"I could tie knots in the straps," said Atticus. "But on this road I'd feel safer with a new harness."

"There are stables in the village up ahead," said Jonathan. "In a few miles the road becomes too narrow for carriages anyway. The guidebook says you can hire mules for the ascent to Delphi."

"We don't need to hire mules," said Flavia. "We have our own. Atticus, will you stay here and guard the carruca while Nikos goes to the village to get someone from one of the stables to come look at it? If they repair it we can pick it up on our way back. Meanwhile, the four of us will ride the mules up to Delphi. Today's the day of the oracle, and I'm sure Aristo will be there. If we don't go now, we might miss him."

"You want me to go to the village alone?" asked Nikos in a small voice.

"You can share one of our mules as far as the village," said Flavia. "On the way back, you can keep Tigris with you as your protector. Is that all right, Jonathan?"

"Yes," said Jonathan. "That's fine."

"That sounds like a plan, Miss Flavia," said Atticus, "but where will Nikos and Tigris and I meet you once we've dealt with the carriage?"

"Do you know any good taverns or guesthouses in Delphi?"

"Don't know. It's been a long time since I was last here. Back then I stayed in the campsite on the slopes below Athena's sanctuary. Couldn't afford to stay in a proper inn."

Jonathan reached into the back of the carruca. "The guidebook recommends an inn," he said. "Here it is: a high-quality hospitium beside the famous Castalian Spring, right on the main road."

"Good," said Flavia, looking over his shoulder. "It's got the courtyard symbol so it must have a kitchen and stables." She looked at Nikos and Atticus. "I'll try to reserve rooms and we'll all meet there for dinner. Does it have a name, Jonathan?"

He nodded. "The Castalian Inn."

"Clouds are like fog," said Nubia over her shoulder as they emerged from a cloud and began the descent to Delphi. "Just fog."

"What did you think they'd be like?" said Flavia, who was riding behind her.

The four mules were roped together in a line, with Nubia leading the way on Piper. Flavia followed on Cuminum and the boys took up the rear on Cinnamum and Coriandrum. Like the girls, they wore their packs and used blankets as saddles.

"I thought clouds would be sharp when you enter and exit them," said Nubia. "Like egg whites when Alma whips them up stiff. But they are fuzzy and damp."

As they descended the narrow rocky road, they met more and more people coming the opposite way. A Roman lady carried by a four-man litter stopped to tell them that the Pythia was in fine form. They showed her the portrait of Aristo, but she hadn't seen him. However, many other Greek pilgrims nodded vigorously when Lupus showed his portrait, and they pointed back the way they had come.

"Apollo! Apollo!" said several of them.

"Not far away," said a large man on a tiny donkey. "He is there! He is there!"

"According to this book we should have arrived by now," said Jonathan, as their mules rounded a bend in the narrow road.

"Aaah!" cried Lupus, and pointed up.

Nubia followed his pointing finger and a thrill of awe made her shiver. Above the tops of the tallest pines and almost touching the low clouds was the colossal head and shoulders of a bronze giant. The towering statue showed a beautiful young man with smooth cheeks and curly hair. His eyes seemed to gaze over all of Greece. It was Apollo, the Far-Shooter, and he looked exactly like Lupus's portrait of Aristo.

■ ■ ■

"Oh, Pollux, Pollux, Pollux!" cursed Flavia. "All those people thought we meant Apollo, not Aristo. I thought we almost had him!"

"Well," said Jonathan. "We're here now, so we may as well look for him."

"Of course we'll look for him," she snapped. Her bottom was sore from Cuminum's bumping, and although she wasn't hungry, she felt hollow and dizzy.

Jonathan sighed. "Anyway, that's the sanctuary of Athena down there," he said, pointing toward the slope on the left of the road, "where you can see the little round temple and the big gymnasium."

"Behold the deep valley and far-distant sea," murmured Nubia.

"And this," said Jonathan, gesturing toward a roofed-off section of the rock face on the other side of the road, "must be the Castalian Spring. Any murderers who wash here are cleansed of their pollution."

"Stop!" cried Flavia. "Let's see if anyone has seen a murderer being cleansed of pollution. Nubia! How do I stop this thing?"

Nubia pulled up Piper, and Cuminum and the other mules automatically slowed to a halt too. In the sudden silence Flavia could hear the musical trickle of water off to her right.

"Help," said Flavia, a moment later. She had swung one of her legs over the mule and was now on her stomach, looking over the creature's back with her legs dangling over one side.

"We've got you," came Jonathan's voice from behind her. "Just slide down. . . ." She felt his hands on one leg and Nubia's on the other, so she let herself slip off the mule.

"Ow!" she cried as her feet jarred the ground. "These beasts are taller than they look." She limped toward the roofed springhouse and peered in through the columns. "I can see steps leading down to basins cut in the rock," she said, "but there's nobody here." She turned toward them. "We'll have to ask in the sanctuary. Let's find that hospitium you were telling us about and see if they'll take these mules. I am not riding one more inch."

Lupus grunted and pointed.

"You're right, Lupus," said Jonathan. "It must be that wooden building just behind those pine trees."

"Good," said Flavia. "I hope all those people we saw going the other way means they have some vacancies."

"Yes, please!" cried a shopkeeper in Latin. "Buy your votive gifts here! Figures in bronze, silver, and gold. Clay, too, if your purse is flat."

Half an hour earlier, they had stabled their mules and reserved two rooms at the Castalian Inn. Flavia had given her friends only as much time as they needed to drop their knapsacks and use the latrine before hurrying them up a well-beaten path through the pines and olives to the temenos.

Emerging from the trees, they all stopped to stare at the sanctuary spreading up the steep slope to their right. In the pearly light of an overcast afternoon they saw hundreds of statues and dozens of temples. Dominating them all was the colossal bronze statue of Apollo.

Now, as they passed through a row of Roman-looking shops that flanked the approach to the sanctuary, they were greeted by cries from the shopkeepers.

"Dream garlands!" called one of the shopkeepers from his wide doorway beyond the columns. "Made of sacred bay leaves for lucky dreams! Get your dream garlands here!"

"Guidebooks and maps!" cried the shopkeeper next to him in a husky voice. "Lists of questions to ask the oracle. Descriptions of every monument. Comedies and tragedies."

"Love potions! Curse tablets!" cried a female shopkeeper. "Make him love you and curse his girlfriend! Get them here!"

"Hot sausages! Hot spiced sausages!" The owner of a cookshop came out from between two columns rolling sizzling sausages in an iron pan. "Hot sausages!"

"Oh, Flavia, please for the love of God," whispered Jonathan. "They smell so good and I'm starving."

Flavia bought four spiced sausages—each wrapped in a bay leaf—and was handing them out when a cheerful voice said, "Hello, children! You want guide to the sanctuary? I know everything. I be your personal guide for only one silver coin. I am Mystagogus."

He was a cheerful young man of about Aristo's age.

"Thank you, Mystagogus," said Flavia, taking a tiny bite of her hot sausage, "but we're in a hurry. We don't want a tour. We want to find a fugitive."

"I help you find fugitive," said the youth. He had round cheeks, a snub nose, and coarse wavy hair the color of old straw. "I am Mystagogus. I speak the Latin very good," he said. "I answer all your questions. I help you find all fugitives." He showed his dimples, and Flavia was reminded of the statue of a laughing faun she had once seen.

"All right," she said. "If you can answer a question, then you can be our guide."

The young man raised his pale eyebrows at Jonathan and said, "This one is your sister? Girlfriend, maybe? Very bold young Roman girl."

Jonathan almost choked on his mouthful of sausage.

"Where," said Flavia, ignoring his remarks, "is the fugitive who tried to kill my father?"

The smile faded from the youth's round face. "This I cannot tell you. This is question for the Pythia. But today she has very long line and it is now late in the day."

"If you can't answer my question, then you can't be our guide." Flavia hooked her arm through Nubia's and pushed past him.

"Wait!" cried Mystagogus. "I suddenly think I know the answer!"

Flavia stopped and turned.

"At noon today," he said, "comes a man running through crowds. He has two, maybe three days of beard and torn tunic. His eyes they are wild and red. His hair is like this!" He ruffled his coarse hair and adopted a wild-eyed look. "Maybe these stains on his tunic are old blood." Mystagogus pointed at imaginary spots on his own tunic. "Maybe this is the man you seek?"

"Yes!" cried Flavia. "Lupus! Show him the picture!"

Lupus nodded, chomped a last piece of sausage, threw his whole head back, swallowed like a dog, and then took out his wax tablet. Mystagogus was staring at Lupus open-mouthed.

"Don't look at him!" said Flavia. "Look at the picture."

Mystagogus squinted down at the wax tablet and his face lit up. "Yes! That is the man. Though he looks not as divine as your tablet shows."

"Can you take us to him?"

"Of course." The youth bowed. "I am Mystagogus. I am your Delphi guide."

SCROLL XIV

"Can't we go any faster?" asked Flavia, tapping the guide's shoulder.

"As you see," Mystagogus gestured with both arms, "today are many people on the sacred way. The Pythia sits on her tripod and so the sanctuary path is crowded." He turned and shuffled backward, so that he was facing them. "Do not worry, we will arrive. We will arrive. Meanwhile you may ask me any questions."

"What are all these marbles and bronzes?" asked Nubia, gesturing at the forest of statues, columns, altars, and miniature temples around them.

"Most statues are private dedications to the god. The altars are for fulfilment of vow. The small buildings are treasure houses of many cities across the world." Mystagogus spread his arms wide. "Whenever a city wants to thank Apollo the Far-Shooter for answered prayer or his special favor, they build a treasure house and put in it the gifts they promised to give him. Athletes who maybe win olive crown in Olympia or kings who vanquish their foe cannot afford a whole house, so they set up merely a statue."

"Look at that giant three-headed snake, Nubia," said Jonathan.

She shuddered. "It is as tall as that golden palm tree."

"Look over there, Lupus," said Jonathan, "there's a bronze statue of a dolphin. And there's a wolf, too."

"Sometimes wolves still come down from the slopes of Parnassus in the winter," said Mystagogus. He gestured toward the rugged, pine-clad slopes looming above them. "That is Parnassus, you know."

Ahead of them a group of Ethiopians had stopped, and they heard the guide saying, "This is the most famous treasury in Delphi. It was once estimated that the goods inside are worth six hundred million sesterces."

"Has anyone ever tried to rob the treasuries?" asked Jonathan in a whisper.

"Many times," said Mystagogus, as they moved forward again. "But the god always protects what is his. For example, Nero Caesar takes many statues. That is why you see these naked plinths. But Nero dies soon after. Other time a thief steals gold from this treasury my colleague is now describing. This thief runs up to woods on Parnassus. But a wolf finds this thief and kills him and howls until people come to discover all the gold. That is why they make statue of the wolf."

"But where is the altar of Apollo?" asked Flavia. "Where will the fugitive be?"

"It is there, in the great temple of Apollo!" said Mystagogus as they rounded a bend in the path. "Do you see the letters written there? 'GNOTHI SEAUTON.' Do you know what means 'gnothi seauton'?"

Jonathan nodded. "It means 'Know yourself.'"

"Oh!" cried Mystagogus, looking at Nubia. "This one is very clever! He is maybe your boyfriend?" He winked at her.

"I'm interested in philosophy," said Jonathan.

"And I'm interested in catching the man who tried to kill my father," snapped Flavia. "Just take us to the temple."

Mystagogus bowed in mock humility, winked at Lupus, and

gestured for them to ascend the marble steps. The Ethiopians dispersed from around an object in the temple forecourt. Now, as their guide moved them on, Flavia stared. It looked like the top half of a huge marble egg. It was decorated with a strange relief pattern, and it sat on a painted base.

"The omphalos," said Jonathan.

"What are those bumps on it?" asked Nubia.

"It is a carving of, how should we say, net made with locks of hair," said Mystagogus. "This altar is the omphalos. It shows that here, this temple of Apollo where you are now standing, is the very center of the world."

"Bad news, Miss Roman Girl," said Mystagogus, emerging from the temple a few moments later. "The man seeking sanctuary is not the one you want."

"What?" asked Flavia.

Mystagogus drew them down the steps of the temple and off the path to a space between an oleander bush and an iron sculpture of Hercules and the hydra. "The priests tell me that the man who came earlier was fratricide."

"What is fratricide?" asked Nubia.

"It's a Greek word," said Flavia. "It means a person who kills his brother."

Nubia's eyes widened. "Greeks have a special word for someone who kills his brother?"

"Are they sure the man was a fratricide?" Flavia asked Mystagogus.

"They are sure. He is confessing, saying, 'I am sorry! I killed my own brother! I didn't mean to do it! The Kindly Ones pursue me!' and other such things."

Jonathan raised an eyebrow. "You're telling us that the wild-eyed man in a bloodstained tunic who came here is a different one from *our* wild-eyed man in a bloodstained tunic?"

"Yes, Young Roman Boy. That is exactly what I am saying."

"Do you get a lot of bloodstained murderers coming through?" asked Jonathan drily.

Mystagogus nodded cheerfully. "At least one or two a month," he said. "Even more when the south wind blows."

They all stared at him, and Lupus mouthed the word: What?

"The south wind," said Mystagogus. "You Romans call it the *Africus*. It was blowing here two nights ago, and probably elsewhere, too. They say that when *Africus* blows, men cannot be held accountable for their actions."

"You know," said Flavia slowly. "I'm sure the *Africus* was blowing in Corinth the night Aristo attacked Pater. Remember the warm wind that kept banging the shutters?"

"Yes," said Nubia, "I remember."

"Have there been any other bloodstained fugitives coming through today?" asked Jonathan.

"No," said Mystagogus firmly. "I would know. Mystagogus knows everything that goes on at Delphi."

"Then that bloodstained man *must* have been Aristo," said Flavia. Suddenly her eyes widened. "Great Juno's peacock! Maybe Aristo is Pater's brother!"

"What? How? What?" Jonathan asked.

"Maybe Pater and Uncle Gaius had a younger brother who was stolen by slave dealers in infancy and brought to Greece, and Pater never told me because he thought it might upset me."

They all looked at her.

"Oh, I don't know!" Flavia closed her eyes and rested her forehead on the cold marble base of the statue. "All the clues are tangled together in my head like a ball of wool. Only the gods could unravel them. That's it!" she cried suddenly, lifting her head and turning to look at them. "Mystagogus! Can you get me an audience with the Pythia? I could ask her why Aristo tried to kill Pater and how to lift the curse!"

"I am sorry," said the guide. "First of all, women and girls are not allowed to visit the Pythia. But even if you could, it is almost dusk." He gestured toward the temple. "You can see how long is the line of people. Many will be turned away."

"But I *have* to ask her. I'm sure she would have the answer."

"What about all these many people who have come so far to see her?" asked Nubia.

"They must go home disappointed," said Mystagogus, "or wait here until the seventh day of the next month."

For several moments they stared silently at the crowd of people waiting on the temple steps.

"See there?" Mystagogus pointed. "The priests are already sending people at bottom of line away. The precinct closes at sunset."

"Mystagogus," said Jonathan suddenly, "were you born here in Delphi?"

"Of course." The young man bowed. "I am Mystagogus, your Delphi guide."

"And have you ever had an audience with the oracle?"

"Me myself?" he said in surprise. "No, no, no." He showed his dimples. "Give me enough silver to buy bread and cheese and wine and I am perfectly content. There are no mysteries in Mystagogus's life!" He giggled at his own joke.

"According to my guidebook," Jonathan tapped his codex, "natives of Delphi have something called *promanteia*."

"What is pro man tee uh?" said Nubia.

"It means they can go straight to the front of the line," said Jonathan. "Anybody born in Delphi can see the Pythia without waiting."

"If only the Pythia will answer my question," sighed Flavia a half hour later. "I might be able to save Pater."

They were seated on the wooden terrace of the Castalian Inn, sipping honeyed barley water and waiting for the return of Mysta-gogus. Atticus and Nikos had been waiting when they arrived, and Tigris had greeted his young master with ecstatic barks.

"This is a most beautiful inn," said Nubia, "and a most beautiful sunset!" She looked up at the mountains of Delphi rearing around them, their rounded peaks golden in the light of the sinking sun. The clouds were moving east, and the clear sky to the west was tinted with bands of orange and yellow. "This place," she added, "has something magical about it."

"Yes," said Flavia. "I think that's the presence of the god, the Far-Shooter. We have a word for it: numinous."

"Numinous," whispered Nubia, tasting the sound of the word. "Yes, this place is numinous." She stood up and went to the wooden rail. Below her the pine-dotted cliffs tumbled steeply down toward the little sanctuary of Athena. On the green slopes below she could see tents peeping between the olives and pines—a semipermanent campsite for poorer pilgrims. "I feel small here," said Nubia, "but also," she groped for the word, "precious. I feel that something important wants to happen here."

"To you?" said Jonathan, looking up from a slender papyrus codex.

"To all of us."

A haunting cry echoed in the crystal clear air above them.

"Look!" cried Flavia. "An eagle!"

"I think he is a kind of hawk," said Nubia.

"Yes, it's a hawk," said Jonathan, and returned to his codex.

"It's flying on our left!" said Flavia.

"Is that good?" whispered Nubia.

Flavia nodded. "It's a very good omen," she said. "I think you're right, Nubia. Something good is about to happen."

"Hey!" said Atticus. "Where's Lupus?"

"I think he went to the latrine," said Nikos.

"But that was ages ago," said Flavia.

Jonathan looked up from his book and frowned. "So where is he?"

The sun had just set as Lupus slipped out of the latrines of the Castalian Inn and wove through the pines in the direction of the temenos. Out of the corner of his eye he caught a movement high in the air: something as dark and silent as a flake of soot but flitting like a moth. It was a bat.

Lupus smiled. He liked bats. They were small, fast, unpredictable, and virtually invisible. He would be like a bat now. Difficult to see in the fading light of dusk. He peeped around a smooth marble column at the entrance to the Roman Market. Most shops were now shuttered, but one or two had torches burning in their brackets, so he took no chances. He ran fast and low, stopping every so often to press himself against one of the columns of the portico.

When he reached the main gates of the sanctuary, he found the priest ushering out the last pilgrims. No entry there. But that was no problem. Only last month he had crept into another sanctuary of Apollo, the one on the island of Rhodes. All he needed was a tree beside the sanctuary wall. And there were plenty of trees here in Delphi.

As he moved up the steep hillside, he thought about the sanctuary on Rhodes and the battle of wits he had fought there with a criminal mastermind. He remembered the white-haired priestess who had told him that his mother was alive, but that he could not see her because she had dedicated herself to the service of Apollo. He remembered the dream he had dreamed that night in the sanctuary of Rhodes: a dream in which his mother had come to him and held him and sung softly to him in Greek. But in the morning there had been no trace of her, and the white-haired priestess told him she had been sent far away to another sanctuary of Apollo.

Lupus paused beside a tree to catch his breath. There were hundreds of sanctuaries to the Far-Shooter; he couldn't visit them all. But the Pythia might be able to tell him which sanctuary his mother had been sent to, and she might not even have to breathe the sweet fumes from the crevice to do it.

Mystagogus had told them that the Pythia never saw women or girls, but he hadn't said anything about boys. Lupus knew exactly where she would be: in the Temple of Apollo, seeing Mystagogus, her final client of the day.

Lupus studied the tree beside him. It was a laurel—the tree sacred to Apollo. It was close to the wall and perfect for climbing.

Before he went up it, Lupus touched the wax tablet at his belt to make sure it was safe. On it he had carefully written his question for the Pythia:

IN WHICH OF APOLLO'S SANCTUARIES IS MY
MOTHER, MELISSA OF SYMI?

SCROLL XV

As Lupus dropped from a pine branch into the sanctuary, his right foot slipped on a pine cone and he gave an involuntary cry. He had twisted the same ankle the previous month, and it was still tender. He paused, holding his breath, waiting for the guards to seize him.

Nothing. No sound. Just an owl hooting softly in the violet dusk. He gave a slow sigh of relief and looked around. He had landed beside a small marble altar that still bore the messy remains of someone's sacrifice. He moved away from the smell and peered around a granite statue base. The temple of Apollo rose up directly before him. He was surprised to see it closed and dark, apart from a torch on either side of the firmly shut double doors. Wasn't this where Mystagogus was having his audience with the Pythia?

He cautiously crossed the path and limped up the marble steps, past the omphalos to the huge bronze doors, with their lattice-work pattern. Peering inside, he could see one flickering torch, but nothing else. Beyond was darkness.

The disappointment struck him like a blow to the stomach. If the Pythia wasn't here, where could she be?

■ ■ ■

"Mystagogus!" Flavia jumped up from the table as their guide appeared in the doorway of the dining room. "Did they let you see the Pythia?"

"Yes, of course," he said, "I am Mystagogus, your Delphi guide; I have *promanteia*!"

"Then come and tell us quickly!"

"Behold!" said Nubia, pointing at the table. "We save you dinner. It is young rooster," she recited, "pressed and seasoned with salt and rosemary. There are mushrooms and artichokes, too."

"Flavia got us this nice table close to the fire," added Jonathan.

"Come," said Atticus, using his foot to push an empty chair out from under the table. "Sit. Eat. Drink." He twisted in his chair. "Waiter," he called, "bring more mulsum!"

"Mystagogus, this is Atticus," said Flavia, "our bodyguard, and that's our friend Nikos. Oh, and that's Tigris."

Mystagogus sat down and nodded at them.

"Did you ask the Pythia my question?" said Flavia, leaning forward. "Tell us what happened!"

"After I present the priest with a *pelanos*, a kind of pie, he takes me to altar, and there I must put my hand upon goat's head."

"Was the money I gave you enough for a goat?"

"Yes. Money was sufficient. Priest takes goat and sprinkles cold water on goat and goat shivers."

"Is that good?"

"If goat does not shiver then no oracle."

"But the goat shivered."

"The goat shivered. Then priest says some words and cuts throat of goat. The other priest helps him to pour blood out on altar. Then other priest stays to cut up goat and first priest leads me into temple."

"Then you saw the Pythia?"

"No. Then they lead me into the inner room of the temple so that it appears I visit Pythia. But from there we descend steps and then go down dark corridor for a long way, perhaps, how do you say, underground. We walk and walk and walk, and presently I perceive the path climbs again. Then I find myself in a cave or, how do you say, chasm. It is dark and damp with two scribes and a curtain beyond. That is where Pythia now prophesies."

"So she's not underneath the temple?"

"Correct," said Mystagogus. "She is not in the temple."

Lupus angrily swiped at the tears in his eyes and leaned back against one of the massive fluted columns. He was too late. The Pythia had gone and he had missed his chance.

Suddenly he heard the crunch of footsteps on the path below him and the sound of someone singing—a boy or a woman. He moved behind the column and peered out.

A pale, slender shape was moving on the same path they had taken earlier that day. The flickering torches on either side of the temple doors showed it was a woman in white with a water jar on her head. Was it the Pythia? No, she seemed too young. She must be a priestess of Apollo.

He could not see her clearly as she moved off into the deep purple dusk, but he could hear her singing in Greek, singing the words of a dimly remembered lullaby: *When you come home, when you come home to me.* Suddenly all the blood in his arms seemed to fall to his fingertips, and he felt the stars above him being sucked into blackness.

Could it be his mother, Melissa?

He took a deep breath, then another, and saw the stars return to their places. He found that he had fallen to his knees beside the omphalos. He stood on trembling legs and waited for his heart to slow a little. Then he limped out from behind the egg-shaped altar, quietly descended the stairs, and followed the ghostly white shape of the priestess as she moved up the curving path toward the fountain.

As he followed her between statues and altars his mind raced. How could it be his mother? Of all the sanctuaries in all the world, what were the chances of him finding her here? And yet . . . This was Apollo's greatest sanctuary, and she had dedicated her life to that god. His heart was racing as fast as a rabbit's but as he rounded a curve in the sacred path, it almost stopped.

In the murky dusk before him crouched a fully armed soldier, his sword out and ready, his shield in his left hand, and his eyes glinting with malice.

"How do you see the Pythia if she's behind a curtain?" Flavia asked Mystagogus.

"You don't. But I have seen them before. They are woman of about fifty years old with gray hair and looking most ordinary."

"They? I thought there was only one."

"No. There are three of them."

"Three Pythias?"

"It is tired work. When one exhausts the next takes over. They take turns."

"But you asked her the question."

"Yes. The priest made me write out the question on a thin piece of lead. Then he reads it loudly outside curtain."

"Did he read the question exactly as I wrote it?"

Mystagogus put down his piece of rooster and reached into his belt pouch. He pulled out the scrap of papyrus with Flavia's question.

HOW CAN THE ROMAN GIRL FLAVIA GEMINA UNDO THE CURSE WHICH ARISTO FROM THE TOWN OF CORINTH PUT ON HER FATHER BEFORE HE TRIED TO KILL HIM?

"The priest used my exact words?"

"Yes," said Mystagogus, taking a sip of mulsum. "He asks it in loud voice. I hear priestess murmuring behind her curtain, and then I smell something sweet that makes me little bit dizzy. These are the fumes from the rock."

"And then? What did the Pythia say?" Flavia asked Mystagogus. "Tell us, please!"

Mystagogus smiled, wiped his mouth with his cloak, and took a parchment scroll from a cloth belt pouch. It was the size of his index finger and tied with a red ribbon. "She speaks most softly," he said, as he extended the scroll, "so it was difficult to understand her. But the two priests speak one to the other and then they write the Pythia's answer in Greek hexameter."

"In Greek?" wailed Flavia, taking the parchment.

"Yes, but they also translate it into Latin, as you see."

A frown creased Flavia's forehead as she pulled off the ribbon and read what was written on the parchment.

"What does it say?" asked Nikos.

"Read it out loud, Flavia!" said Jonathan.

"Yes, read it," said Nubia.

Flavia looked up at them and then back down at the parchment. Then she read it.

"For Flavia Gemina. Ponder the god's answer and act wisely: "No man or woman has ever tried to kill your father, And no one ever will. Polydeuce's brother will live long and prosper, And he will regain his reason on the day it rains from a clear sky."

Flavia turned to Mystagogus, "But it doesn't say anything about Aristo or the curse!" she cried. "It's nonsense! It's just wool fluff!"

Lupus froze, muscles coiled, waiting to see which way the guard would go. The soldier's eyes glared out at Lupus from the eyeholes of his bronze Corinthian helmet, but he remained perfectly immobile. He was obviously going to let Lupus make the first move.

With his ankle twinging, Lupus knew it would be difficult to outrun the guard. But not impossible. So he feinted right, then left, ready to move in the opposite direction the soldier might go. But the soldier was not fooled. He remained frozen in his crouched position, still as a statue.

Abruptly, Lupus realized that he *was* a statue.

He felt the hot rush of blood to his cheeks, and he was glad no one had seen him make a fool of himself. Silently cursing his own stupidity, Lupus brought his face close to the statue's and looked into the eyeholes of the helmet. The statue's eyes were probably made of some semiprecious stone, highly polished to make them look wet. Lupus slowly put his forefinger through the eyehole of the helmet and touched the glistening eyeball, just to be sure. Yes, it was made of cold, smooth stone.

Lupus patted the statue on its bronze shoulder and limped up the path after the priestess with the jar.

SCROLL XVI

"Lukos!" The water jar fell and shattered as it struck the granite lip of the fountain. "Oh, Lukos, my son!" Now his mother's arms were around him, smooth and cool and strong. He could smell her scent: honey and pine.

"Oh, thank you, Apollo!" she cried. "Thank you for bringing my precious son to me." She hugged him tightly, then pushed him away and gazed down at him. "Open your mouth," she whispered. "I must see. No, it's too dark. Come up here!" She took his hand and pulled him almost roughly along the path and back up the steps of the temple to where the torches burned.

Standing beside the massive columns in the flickering golden light, he saw her dear, beautiful face—the face he thought he had forgotten—now perfectly familiar again.

She held the sides of his head in her cool hands and tipped his face up and made him open his mouth; she gazed inside. Then she threw back her head and wailed. There was so much anguish in her cry that Lupus began to sob, too. Not for himself, but for her.

"The Pythia's answer is nonsense!" repeated Flavia Gemina in disgust, throwing the parchment scroll down onto the table. "Utter wool fluff!"

"It is not the Pythia's answer," said Mystagogus. "But Apollo's."

Jonathan picked up the parchment.

"Read it again," said Atticus.

"No man or woman has ever tried to kill your father,"
read Jonathan,

"And no one ever will. Polydeuces's brother will live long and prosper. And he will regain his reason on the day it rains from a clear sky."

He raised his eyebrows at Flavia.

"What does it mean?" Nikos frowned.

"It is ambiguous," said Nubia.

"It's not ambiguous!" cried Flavia. "It's wool fluff!"

"Yet this is how the oracle always speaks," said Mystagogus. "In riddles."

"Waiter!" called Atticus. "Bring us more mulsum! Hot and spiced, and well-watered for the children. Now, let's study this line by line. You have to know how to interpret these things. Read it again, Jonathan?"

"No man or woman has ever tried to kill your father . . ." began Jonathan.

"See?" said Flavia, swallowing angry tears. "Right away they got it wrong. So how can we believe the rest? It's all nonsense. I spent the last of our money from Pater's strongbox on a goat for that stupid oracle and on the rooms at this inn. I don't even know if we can afford to go back to Corinth now. It's been three days and who knows what's happened to Pater! Maybe his wounds have festered and maybe he's . . . Now we'll never catch Aristo or find out how to undo the curse."

Flavia felt the ache in her throat as she tried to fight back hot tears. Nubia's arm was around her and someone put a warm beaker between her hands. She took a sip of the spicy liquid. It was good. Beneath the table she suddenly felt Tigris's tail thumping against her feet, and she looked up to see Lupus standing in the doorway.

He had a strange look on his face, as if he had just seen something miraculous.

111

"Master Lupus!" cried Atticus. "Where have you been? Are you all right?"

Lupus limped forward, as if in a trance, and he put his wax tablet carefully on the table.

Jonathan picked it up and his eyes widened as he read it. "You found out what the Pythia told the fugitive? And where he's gone? But how?"

Lupus took his bronze stylus and leaned over the wax tablet on the table.

A PRIESTESS TOLD ME he wrote, and his hand trembled as he added two final words: MY MOTHER.

The waiter brought warm honey cakes as they questioned Lupus. By asking questions requiring the answer yes or no, and with some help from gestures, and a few words scribbled on his tablet, they learned that he had been hiding in the precinct when he saw a priestess and heard her singing a familiar song. When he caught up with her at the fountain, she recognized him at once. She knew he was in Delphi but because she could not leave the temenos, she had asked the god to bring Lupus to her.

"How did she even know you were here?" asked Flavia.

REMEMBER PHRIXUS? wrote Lupus on his tablet.

"Phrixus?" said Jonathan. "The slave who was with old Pliny when he died?"

Lupus grunted yes.

"The slave who is being set free by young Pliny?" asked Nubia.

Lupus grunted yes again, and wrote:

HE STOPPED IN SYMI LAST MONTH, ON THE WAY

TO ALEXANDRIA. HE FOUND MY MOTHER AND
TOLD HER HOW VENALICIUS DIED. HE TOLD HER
ABOUT ALL OF YOU AND WHEN SHE HEARD THE
PYTHIA TALKING ABOUT THE QUESTION ASKED BY
A GIRL NAMED FLAVIA GEMINA—

"She knew you would probably be here with me!" cried Flavia.
Lupus nodded.

"Did you ask her about Aristo?"

Lupus grunted yes. He told them how, in the torchlight of the
temple of Apollo, he had shown his mother the picture of Aristo
painted on the back of his tablet.

"That's the man your friend Flavia wanted to know about?" she
said. "The bad man who hurt her father? All the other priestesses
are talking about him."

Lupus nodded.

"The other priestesses say a man came to the sanctuary around
noon today. He was clinging to the omphalos in the forecourt and
babbling about the Kindly Ones. He began to alarm the tourists
and pilgrims. So the priests took him and bathed him in the
Castalian Spring and gave him fresh clothes and then took him in
to see the Pythia." She lowered her voice even more. "Did you
know she prophesies from a chasm?"

Lupus shook his head.

"An earthquake closed the vent beneath the god's temple during the reign of Tiberius. For several years the Pythia was dumb.
She could not prophesy. Then they discovered another vent. It
took them a long time to build the tunnel. The fumes there are
not as good. Some say the god does not speak through her anymore, but I believe he does."

Lupus nodded, looking up into her beautiful face framed by
honey-colored hair.

"Now I will tell you what she told the fugitive." His mother glanced around, then put her mouth so close to his ear that he could feel her soft, warm breath. "The oracle told the fugitive that his case would be heard in the city of Orestes' trial, that he would face his accuser in the House of the Maiden, and that he would receive the verdict in the Cave of the Kindly Ones."

His mother's eyes filled with tears, and she kissed his forehead. "The man who hurt Flavia's father left this evening. If you are to help her, my dear son, then you must depart at dawn tomorrow."

In the torchlit dining room of the Castalian Inn, they all stared at Lupus.

"Oh, Lupus," cried Nubia, "I am so happy you find your mother at last."

Lupus nodded and lowered his eyes. He had not told them everything. He had not told them how his mother dropped her water jug when she saw him and how she had wailed when she gazed into his tongueless mouth. He did not tell them all the things she had whispered in his ear and how she had covered his face with kisses, weeping all the time. He did not tell them that she was learning to read and write and that she had taken his wax tablet and written the words

I LOVE YOU in trembling Greek.

"Thank you, Lupus," said Flavia, giving him a quick hug. "For leaving your mother to tell us where Aristo has gone. But where has he gone?" She looked at his wax tablet and read, "The site of Orestes' trial, the House of the Maiden, the Cave of the Kindly Ones . . ."

"Athens," said Jonathan. "He's gone to Athens."

"Of course," cried Flavia. "The Maiden's House is the Parthenon on the Acropolis: the temple of Athena, who is also known as the Maiden."

"I think the site of Orestes' trial was the Areopagus," said Atticus. "A hill just below the Acropolis."

Jonathan nodded. "That's where the Cave of the Kindly Ones is, and it's where Orestes was finally judged after he murdered his mother."

"How do you know that?" cried Flavia. "Even I didn't know that."

"I've been doing research," he said with a smile, and tapped his papyrus codex. "Aeschylus," he said. "*The Eumenides*. I bought it in the Roman market while you were haggling for the sausages."

"Oh, thank you, Castor and Pollux," breathed Flavia, lifting her face to the ceiling. "Thank you!" She opened her eyes and looked at the others. "We'll need to raise some money. I think we'll have to sell two of the mules—"

"No!" cried Nubia. "Not the mules! They have been most faithful."

"Can you think of another way to raise money by tomorrow?" Flavia looked around the table.

"Yes," said Nubia. "We can sell carruca."

"That's not a bad idea, Miss Flavia," said Atticus. "With its new harness, the carruca will fetch quite a nice price. We could ride the mules, doubling up. It will only take us half the time to reach Athens as it would have done traveling in the carriage."

"You mean ride on their backs?" said Flavia in a small voice.

"Yes. But if we leave at dawn and ride hard we might reach Athens by tomorrow evening."

"Well," Flavia sighed, "we'd better go to sleep then. Especially as we're leaving at dawn."

Lupus stood and shook his head.

"What?" cried Flavia. "You're coming with us, aren't you?"

Lupus nodded.

"You *are* coming with us?"

Lupus nodded again and bent forward to write on his tablet.

BUT TONIGHT I MUST RETURN TO MY MOTHER. SHE IS WAITING FOR ME.

■ ■ ■

They left Delphi at the first light of dawn on the following day. Nubia and Flavia rode Piper at the front, followed by Jonathan and Nikos, who each had a mule to themselves, but had to carry the blankets and backpacks. Atticus and Lupus took up the rear on Cinnamum. Lupus had spent all night in the temenos with his mother. He was too exhausted to answer their eager questions and had fallen asleep almost instantly. Now his head lolled back on Atticus's shoulder.

The day was overcast but warm, and from the trees on either side of the road came a torrent of birdsong. The mules' hooves beat a steady rhythm on the packed earth road. Flavia and her friends had to raise their voices to be heard as they greeted approaching pilgrims and asked if they had passed a certain man on the road.

Lupus heard none of it. He half woke when they stopped for lunch outside Thebes, but he fell asleep as soon as they set off again and he did not completely revive until the sun was low in the sky.

"Oh!" groaned Flavia, splashing her feet in the stream. "I've never been so stiff and sore in my entire life."

"If you think it's bad now," said Atticus, "just wait until tomorrow. You'll be in agony."

They had stopped to water the mules at a clear stream near a village beyond a ruined fortress, when Lupus had kicked off his sandals and plunged in, tunic and all. Jonathan and Tigris had joined him, but Flavia and Nikos found a grassy patch under a tall poplar tree.

"This is as good a place to camp as any," said Atticus. "Water and shelter if it rains. I think I'll walk into the village for some bread and maybe cheese."

"Aren't you going to ride?" said Flavia. They looked over toward the mules, tethered to three poplar trees farther down the stream. Nubia had taken off their packs and was stroking them with the flat of her hand.

"I'll walk," said Atticus. "I've had enough of riding mules for one day. Especially with a sleeping nine-year-old in my arms."

Flavia smiled at Nikos as Atticus limped off toward the road. A plate of clouds had covered the sky since noon, but now the sun sank below it and sent its slanting golden light to make the leaves of the trees glow like emeralds.

"Good swim?" said Flavia to Lupus as he splashed out of the stream and came toward them. "Do you feel better?"

Lupus nodded and gave her a thumbs-up. He went to the pile of luggage by the mules, found a rolled-up blanket, brought it back, and unfurled it on a sunny spot in the grass beside them.

Jonathan flopped down beside him, soaking wet and wheezing a little, and a moment later Tigris ran up and shook himself off.

"No, Tigris!" giggled Nikos. "Don't do that right here!"

"He always does that," said Nubia, coming up to join them. She put down their knapsacks and Jonathan's bow and arrows. "He be-spatters the tunics." She spread her palla beside the boys' blanket, and sat facing the west with her eyes closed, letting the sunshine warm her face.

"Why don't you and Nikos come into sun?" she said to Flavia. "It is most wonderful."

"No, thank you," said Flavia. "I'm getting horribly tanned as it is. I don't want to look like a field slave."

"I got sunburn," said Nikos, "even though it was cloudy most of the day." He pinched his rosy forearm.

"I wonder how much farther it is to Athens?" mused Flavia.

"About twenty-five miles," said Jonathan, "according to the last milestone we passed."

"Can't we make it by this evening?" asked Flavia. "Atticus said we could reach Athens by the evening."

"He said we *might*." Jonathan rolled over onto his stomach and undid his pack and pulled out his guidebook. "Great Neptune's beard," he said a few moments later. "We covered nearly seventy miles today. No wonder we're so exhausted."

"If we've traveled nearly seventy miles," said Flavia, "then why haven't we caught up with him?" She kicked her bare feet furiously in the stream. "This is so frustrating!"

"Flavia," said Jonathan, "it says here that there's a sanctuary to the goddess Demeter at Eleusis, about fifteen miles from here. There's an oracle there, too." He looked up at her. "You don't suppose Aristo would stop to ask another oracle how to be free of the blood guilt, do you?"

"Oh!" groaned Flavia, flopping back on her cloak and looking up at the leaves of the poplar. "I hope not. He got clear instructions from Apollo to go to Athens. But maybe we should go and investigate." Flavia closed her eyes. "Lupus could disguise himself as a beggar boy and sneak in."

"Bad idea," said Jonathan, sitting up. "It says here that the penalty for trespassing is death. Eleusis is the site of the famous Mysteries."

"Oh," said Flavia, and opened her eyes as she felt Lupus tapping her. He was holding his wax tablet inches from her face.

I'M TIRED OF DRESSING UP AS A BEGGAR

"There's nothing wrong with beggars," said Nikos, who had leaned over to read the message. "Beggars help rich people to be generous and comfort the poor by reminding them they could be far worse off."

Flavia saw Lupus narrow his eyes at Nikos.

Jonathan hissed and held up his hand for silence. He was staring out over the meadow, and as they watched he slowly picked his bow and arrow from the grass, took aim at something, and loosed his arrow. "Got it," he muttered, and then: "Fetch, Tigris!"

Tigris sped off silently, and a few moments later he sat beside Jonathan with a dead rabbit in his mouth.

"Good dog," said Jonathan, stroking the glossy black fur on Tigris's head. "Would you sharpen some twigs, Lupus?" he said, as he pulled the arrow out of the rabbit and wiped the shaft on the grass. "If Nubia makes a fire we can have this rabbit cooked by the time Atticus gets back from the village."

Lupus nodded and searched in his knapsack as Nubia cleared a space beneath the spreading branches of a nearby cedar tree.

"Good idea, Nubia," said Jonathan. "If it rains later we'll want to be under cover. Lupus," he said suddenly, "where did you get that knife?"

Lupus stopped sharpening the twig, and a look of alarm flitted across his face. He quickly hid the knife behind his back.

Flavia crawled forward and twisted Lupus's arm so that the knife fell onto the brown blanket. It had an iron blade and an ebony handle set with mother-of-pearl zigzags. As she reached out to pick it up she heard Nikos gasp.

"Where did you get this, Lupus?" said Flavia. "Ugh! There's dried blood here in the cracks between the mother of pearl and the wood."

"Great Jupiter's eyebrows!" exclaimed Jonathan. "It's the murder weapon!"

Flavia screamed and dropped the knife.

"I mean it's the attempted-murder weapon," said Jonathan. "I remember Aristo dropped it, but when I went to look for it the next morning, it had disappeared."

He stretched forward to pick up the knife.

"Lupus!" cried Flavia. "Have you had that since the night of the crime?"

Lupus hung his head and nodded.

"Why didn't you tell us? It could be an important clue!"

Lupus shrugged.

119

"Wanted it for his knife collection, no doubt," said Jonathan to Flavia.

"That is not Aristo's knife," said Nubia, coming up to them. "Aristo has knife with bronze boar's-head handle."

"Maybe he bought a new one," said Flavia.

"I think you're right," said Nikos to Flavia. "I recognize that knife. I mean, I know where he bought it. There's only one shop that sells knives like that."

"Where?" said Jonathan.

"The shop of Pericles the Cutler," said Nikos, "in the town of Corinth."

Lupus looked up as Atticus came across the field from the road. The sun was so low that the shadows of the poplars were twice as long as the trees.

"Well," he said, "they've seen our two fugitives in the village."

"They have?" Flavia jumped up. "Both of them?"

"Both of them," said Atticus. "I didn't have Master Lupus's tablet, but the baker said he saw a young man jogging down the middle of the road twittering to himself, and then an hour later a man who might have been his twin bought some bread and olives. He was riding a donkey."

"When?" cried Flavia.

"Not long. One, maybe two hours ago. He's only one step ahead." Atticus crouched beside the fire and handed some flat bread to Nubia. "Nice fire," he said. "Anyway, I've got some bread. Olives, too." He tossed a papyrus cone onto the blanket.

"Come on!" cried Flavia. "There's no time to eat. Let's go!"

"No, Flavia," said Jonathan. "It took me a long time to catch and skin and gut these rabbits. They'll be done in half an hour."

"But that's too late! It will be dark by then."

"Miss Flavia," said Atticus. "Those mules have put in an extremely long day. So have we. There's no moon to speak of

120

tonight, and it looks like those clouds are coming rather than going. We can't very well carry torches. Besides, I think all of us have lost the feeling in our backsides."

"I know," said Flavia. "I'm sore, too. But it's just so frustrating!" She slumped down again. "He always seems to be just one step ahead."

"Two," said Jonathan, tossing Tigris a piece of offal.

"What?" said Flavia.

"Two steps ahead," repeated Jonathan. "Aristo is two steps ahead and Dion is one step ahead."

"I wish we could at least catch up with Dion," said Flavia. "He might be able to tell us why Aristo did it."

"I'm surprised Dion hasn't caught him by now," said Nikos, through a mouthful of olives, "and that he's riding a donkey. He's won prizes for running at the Isthmian games and could go twice as fast on foot."

"You can't run for three days without a break," said Jonathan.

Nikos nodded. "A few years ago Dion ran all the way from Corinth to Olympia to compete, and the next day he took the prize."

Lupus turned his head to look at Nikos. The boy's pale skin was flushed with sunburn, made even pinker by the light of the setting sun. With his big brown eyes and full lips, he looked almost beautiful. Lupus looked down at Nikos's sandals, neatly placed beside his own, and he noticed with a start that they were the same size.

Suddenly Lupus gasped and sat up straight. He felt as if someone had tipped a bucket of cold water over him.

He knew what was wrong about Nikos.

SCROLL XVII

"Ow!" cried Nikos as Lupus leaned over to poke him in the chest. "That hurt!"

"Lupus!" cried Flavia. "Why did you do that? What's got into you?"

Lupus handed her his skewer, picked up his wax tablet, and wrote:

NIKOS IS A GIRL NOT A BOY

"What?" cried Flavia, reading the tablet. "Nikos is a girl?"

"Ah!" said Nubia.

"Huh?" said Atticus.

"Of *course!*" said Jonathan. "That explains the cloak covering your chest, all those trips to the bushes on your own, and the fact that you scream like a girl."

"I do not scream like a girl," said Nikos, making his voice deep, "because I am not one. I'm a boy and soon I'll be a man."

"Oh, yes?" said Jonathan, handing Atticus his skewered rabbit and rising to his feet. "Then come behind the tree with me and Lupus. Show us your witnesses!"

Lupus nodded and leaped to his feet.

Nikos glared up at the boys. Then his shoulders slumped.

"All right," he said quietly. "You win. I'm a girl."

"I *knew* it!" cried Flavia.

"No, you didn't," said Jonathan. "Lupus figured it out."

"Well then, I suspected it without realizing that I suspected it."

"What is your name?" asked Nubia softly.

"Megara. My name is Megara."

"Like the name of the town we passed through two days ago?" said Jonathan.

"Yes. Like the name of the town."

"You love Dion, don't you?" said Nubia. "That is why you come with us."

Everybody looked at Nubia in amazement; then their heads turned toward Megara.

"Yes. I'm in love with Dion," said Megara at last. "I have been ever since I was your age, Nubia. Ever since I was twelve." She sighed again and shrugged off her cloak, and Lupus chuckled. He could just make out the breasts of Megara, gently swelling beneath her tunic.

"Oh, it's such a relief not to have to pretend anymore," said Megara. She ran her fingers through her feathery dark hair, and Flavia suddenly wondered how she could ever have taken Megara for a boy.

"Why did you disguise yourself as a beggar boy?" asked Jonathan.

"To follow Dion," said Megara. "To help him catch Aristo. To make sure he came to no harm. My parents would never have approved of my going, even with a bodyguard, so I knew I'd have to go without their permission. It's suicide for a woman to travel from Corinth to Athens on her own, so I decided to become a boy." She glanced at Flavia and sighed. "If I'd known how independent Roman girls are, I wouldn't have bothered with this disguise."

123

Jonathan grinned. "Most Roman girls aren't like Flavia," he said.

"What did you do to make yourself a boy?" asked Flavia.

"I chopped off my hair with a knife, and rubbed dirt on my face, and took one of my father's old tunics and our cook's cloak. Also I strapped my breasts, not that they need much strapping."

"I believe some kind of dung was involved, too," said Jonathan.

"Yes, I wanted to smell like a beggar so I rolled in some dried mule dung. Do you think I overdid it?"

"Just a little," said Jonathan. "If you were to take a quick dip in the stream nobody would object."

"I thought if I disguised myself as a beggar boy I'd be safe—it works in the plays . . . but those men . . . If you hadn't saved me when you did, then I don't know what would have happened to me."

"So those men who were hurting you, they guessed you were a woman?" asked Flavia.

"I don't think so," said Megara. "I don't think it would have mattered to them either way."

Flavia shuddered and made the sign against evil. "And you know so much about Aristo and Dion because . . . ?"

"Because I grew up in the house next to them," said Megara.

"I still remember the moment I fell in love with Dion," said Megara. "It was the evening of his fourteenth birthday, four years ago. That was before Aristo went away. I had just turned twelve. Dion's only desire in life was to please his parents. He gave a dinner party for neighbors and family, and after the feast he played a song on the lyre. He had been practicing for months. He played it nicely, but it was a terrible mistake."

"Why?" asked Flavia. The sun had set and in the trees the birds were twittering sleepily.

"Aristo had never even heard the song until that night, but

when Dion finished, he picked up his own lyre and played it again so beautifully that everyone was in tears. Everyone except me."

"How cruel!" said Flavia.

"Yes," said Megara. "Especially as Aristo was always the golden boy and didn't need any more praise. Everything came easily to him: math, poetry, hunting, wrestling, music. Especially music. Poor Dion. . . ." She sighed and gazed into the fire. "The only thing he's good at is running and making furniture. I wasn't invited of course, being a girl, but I was watching from the roof, and I saw his face when Aristo played that song on his lyre. My heart melted for him."

"Does he love you, too?"

"Dion?" Megara dropped her head. "He barely knows I exist. My parents are old fashioned, not like the Roman families in Corinth. They make me stay veiled at home and never let me speak to men. Even if Dion did notice me, he'd never love me. He always likes the wrong ones. The sort of girls who fall in love with Aristo."

"How does Aristo get girls to fall in love with him?" said Flavia. "He hardly spends any time here in Greece. Only a few weeks a year."

"He doesn't need long," said Megara. "Let me tell you what happened this year. A few months ago a girl named Tryphosa moved to our street with her family. She comes from Sparta and she's such a—" Here Megara used a Greek word that Flavia was not familiar with.

Flavia opened her mouth, then shut it again. She could guess what the word meant.

"She's one of those girls who thinks they're far more beautiful than they actually are. She stains her lips pink with blackcurrant juice and never wears a veil and always lets her hair *accidentally* come unpinned and then tosses it around."

125

"That doesn't sound very Spartan," remarked Jonathan. "Aren't the women from Sparta as tough as the men?"

"Don't forget, Jonathan," said Flavia. "The most beautiful woman in the world was from Sparta: Helen of Troy."

"True," said Jonathan, and Atticus chuckled.

"Oh, Tryphosa is very Spartan," said Megara bitterly. "She would always talk about how independent Spartan girls are and then give Dion a long, smoldering look. He swallowed her bait and also her hook and her line." Megara poked the fire with her skewer, watching the branches fizz and hiss. "But I could see she didn't really love him. She just enjoyed the attention and all the gifts he gave her. When Aristo arrived in Corinth a month ago, she took one look at him and licked her berry-stained lips and tossed her hair and went after him."

"Weren't you happy about that?"

Megara nodded. "At first. But Dion was so besotted with Tryphosa that he didn't realize what was happening. She pretended she still loved him, so that he would keep giving her things, but she was secretly seeing Aristo, and he went with her even though he knew Dion loved her."

"Aristo went with Tryphosa?" asked Nubia in a small voice.

Jonathan turned to her. "That means—"

"I know what it means," said Nubia.

"Well," said Jonathan, "Aristo was probably just trying to console himself. He's in love with . . . someone he can't have, too. Back in Italia."

"Aristo in love?" said Megara, arching an eyebrow. "She must be a goddess."

"She's the most beautiful girl you've ever seen," said Flavia. "When men see her their jaws drop and they can't stop staring."

"And she doesn't love Aristo?"

"No," said Flavia. "Anyway, she's married now."

"Ha!" Megara laughed. "Not only beautiful but discerning. It serves Aristo right. The gods do show justice sometimes."

On the other side of the fire, Nubia quietly put down her skewer, rose, and moved away into the green dusk.

"Poor thing," whispered Megara. "It's so obvious she's in love with Aristo, too. Well, she'd better join the crowd."

Nubia found a spot beneath a weeping willow farther up the stream and out of sight of the others. She sat beneath it, looking out through a parting in the curtain of tender green branches. Before her lay a grassy meadow dotted with wildflowers. At the far end of this meadow was a strand of the bushy pines she had come to love, and beyond them lay mountains silhouetted black against a thin green sky, still clear on the horizon. She saw a gust of wind run across the tops of the pines, and by the wavelike ripple of grasses in the meadow she could see it coming toward her. Then the breeze touched her face, and she smelled the fresh, clean smell of coming rain. In the branches above her a dozen tiny birds began squittering with excitement.

"Beautiful, isn't it?" said Aristo's voice.

Nubia turned her head and gasped. Was he a vision or had her longing brought him here?

He stood there in the pearly light, staring toward Athens, showing her his profile. He looked pale and tired and unbearably handsome.

Nubia did not trust her voice, so she nodded. She did not trust her face either, so she turned to look back toward the meadow. He came to sit beside her, not quite touching, but close enough for her to feel the warmth radiating from his shoulder. He was real.

"Flavia thinks I did it, doesn't she?"

Nubia nodded.

He sighed. "That complicates matters. You don't think I did it, do you?"

Nubia shook her head.

"So where are you headed now?"

"We are going to Athens," she said, and was amazed to find her voice sounded normal.

He nodded. "That's what I thought. Tonight?"

"No," said Nubia. "I think we will camp tonight and go tomorrow."

"Praise Apollo!" He breathed a sigh of relief. "That means I'll have time, if I go now. I just need to find him, to find out why." He turned his head and she could feel him looking at her. "Thank you for believing in me," he said softly.

Nubia watched the diaphanous curtain of rain sweeping toward them. It bent the grasses of the meadow, parted the tendrils of the willow, and was suddenly upon them, covering their uplifted faces with a thousand tiny wet kisses. The birds in the tree were pouring down juicy cheeps and behind them the stream chattered with an urgent liquid excitement. Nubia closed her eyes for a moment and then opened them, drinking in the thousand different shades of green before her. Everything was green: the sky, the grass, the trees, the rain. Even the gurgling of the stream and the birdsong sounded green.

"It is green," she said. "So green."

"Yes," he said. "It's green."

They sat quietly together, not speaking, not moving, just staring out at the wet green dusk and letting the billows of rain softly drench them. It felt so natural. Like being with a brother, a friend, someone she had always known.

In that moment Nubia knew that he would always be there, even if she never saw him again in her life. He would always be beside her, watching what she watched, hearing what she heard, knowing without being told what she was thinking and how she was feeling.

■ ■ ■

"Nubia! Where have you been? Are you all right? We were beginning to worry about you. I know you like the rain, but really!
Look at you. You're soaking wet. Come over here by the fire and
put this dry blanket around you. Try some of Jonathan's rabbit. It's
delicious. See? I've been roasting your pieces and they're perfectly
done. Hurry and eat it, because it's almost dark and we need to
get some sleep. Tomorrow we're going to Athens."

Nubia could not sleep. It had stopped raining. Scraps of cloud hurried across the star-filled sky above the canopy of the cedar that
sheltered their campsite. Her heart was filled with joy. Aristo had
trusted her enough to come to her. To her and no one else. *Thank
you for believing in me,* he had said.

She wished she had asked him to tell her what had happened
the night of the attack, so that she could tell Flavia, but sitting
with him in the green rain had been so magical. She hadn't
wanted to break the spell.

If only she were as clever as Flavia, she could work out what
had really happened that night. Then she could tell Flavia and the
others, and they would believe in his innocence, too.

As she gazed up at the lofty dark branches of the cedar, she re-
viewed all the events of the past two days, trying to make sense of
them: Aristo standing over Flavia's father with a bloody knife, his
stunned look, and his silence as the slaves dragged him away.

What else could she remember about that night?

Had he been wearing his red cloak? Yes, draped over his shoulders like a blanket. She hadn't looked at his feet, but she knew
now he must have been barefoot, because later she had found his
red sandals in the other room. If he had been barefoot, wearing
his cloak as a blanket, he must have been in bed when he heard a
noise and—but, no! His was the Orpheus room. Then why was
Captain Geminus in Aristo's bed, with his own sandals under-

neath? And why were Aristo's sandals found in Captain Geminus's room, the room with black walls and little gray sea nymphs swimming around a lower border?

Suddenly she knew the answer. She turned her head, but Flavia was fast asleep: her friend's face was pale in the ruby firelight, and a small frown creased her forehead.

"I will not wake her," thought Nubia. "But I will remember this thing and store it in my heart. It is a clue that will help to prove Aristo is innocent."

Nubia smiled, and presently she slept.

The usual nightmares woke Jonathan before dawn. His lungs were tight and his tunic damp with sweat.

He sat up and groaned because of the stiffness in his limbs. Tigris whined softly and by the red light of the dying embers, Jonathan saw that his dog was standing and looking toward the stream. Over by the poplars, the mules were also awake and restless. He could hear them stamping and snorting.

Jonathan slipped on his sandals. The rain had stopped and in the faint light of the stars he could see tattered clouds drifting across the night sky. He stood and groaned again and limped across the dark slippery grasses toward the black shapes of the poplars. Tigris followed silently. When they reached the mules, Jonathan stroked their necks and backs with long sweeps of his palm, as he had seen Nubia do. Presently they seemed to grow calmer.

He needed to relieve himself and so he limped into the inky shadows of the copse. He had just finished and was about to start back for the campfire, when he heard something like an evil taunting moan coming from the darkness beyond the stream. The sound lifted the little hairs on the back of his neck and arms.

"Lupus?" whispered Jonathan. But he knew it wasn't Lupus. The sound was too distant and now, as it came again, he could tell there was more than one of them.

Beside him a low growl rose in Tigris's throat, and the big puppy moved forward through the black shadows.

"No, Tigris, come back!" whispered Jonathan, his chest tightening. Everything that looked so safe by daylight looked terrifying at night. Was that a person crouching behind that tree? Or just a shrub? Then a new sound came. Not a moan but eerie whoops that faded to evil inhuman laughter. By the sound of it, there were a group of three or four of them, drawing nearer and nearer. He knew what they must be.

The Furies.

His knees grew weak, and he had to clutch a tree trunk to stop himself from collapsing. For a moment he clung to the rough bark and closed his eyes. All those people who had died in the fire in Rome, because of him. And the burning man. His fault, too. Their blood had never been avenged. Now the Furies were after him. They were laughing because he was finally within their grasp.

Tigris whined and moved forward.

"Tigris! Come back!" He heard the wheezing panic in his own voice. The evil echoing laughter came again, just the other side of the stream. He must get away. But as he turned to run, he saw something so terrifying that it stopped his breath.

The creature that stood near the poplar on his side of the stream resembled a muscular woman in a short tunic. It was hard to make out details, but Jonathan knew by her snaky hair gleaming silver in the starlight that she was one of the Furies.

SCROLL XVIII

Jonathan tried to move. The Fury was coming nearer, moving straight toward him. The creature's snaky hair stood out from its head, and now he saw that the Fury carried not a torch, but a bow and quiver. Before him, Tigris was wagging his tail.

"Is that you, Jonathan?" said the Fury in a deep, familiar voice. "Get back to the campfire. There's something very bad out there."

The wave of nausea receded and left Jonathan cold and shivering. "Atticus?" he gasped.

From behind Jonathan came a flickering yellow light. As it grew brighter, it illuminated Atticus's round face and his long, bushy gray hair. Released from its usual ponytail it stood straight out from his head.

"Aaah!" cried Lupus, who had come up beside Jonathan with a flaming branch. Flavia, Nubia, and Megara were close behind him.

"Atticus?" yelped Flavia. "What have you done to your hair?"

"My hair?" Atticus patted his head. "I haven't done anything; just undone the leather strip I tie it back with."

"It's terrifying," said Megara.

"Nothing wrong with my hair," said Atticus. "It's just a little fluffy."

"It is very big," said Nubia. "It resembles evil Medusa hair."

Flavia looked at Nubia, and suddenly the girls began to giggle.

"All right, all right!" Atticus scowled. He handed the bow and quiver to Jonathan, then smoothed his hair back and took a leather thong from his belt. "But listen," he said, as he tied his hair back in its usual ponytail, "we have something more frightening than my hair to worry about."

"What?" said Megara. "What could be more frightening than your hair?"

The inhuman laughter came again, closer than ever.

"What was that?" they cried.

On the other side of the stream, six pairs of eyes glowed yellow in the torchlight.

"Great Juno's peacock!" gasped Flavia. "What are they?"

"I know what they are being," said Nubia. "They are hyenas. They come from my country, from the desert."

"Then what are they doing here?" muttered Jonathan, slipping his quiver over one shoulder and taking out an arrow.

"Probably escaped from the beast fights," said Atticus. "It happens."

Jonathan nocked an arrow. "Are they dangerous, Nubia?"

"Yes," she said. "Do not look at the eyes. Do not let Tigris look at the eyes." She knelt before Jonathan's puppy and covered his eyes.

"Got to look if I'm going to shoot one," muttered Jonathan, pulling back the bowstring until it was tight against his cheek.

The evil cackling came again, and the leader of the pack slowly began to move forward across the stream.

As the lead hyena crossed the stream, Jonathan loosed his arrow.

He already had a second nocked and ready as Flavia cried, "I think you got him!"

The other hyenas moaned and cackled with fear, but they did not retreat. They were moving back and forth on the opposite bank of the stream. They looked like a cross between a hunched dog and a tiger, and in the light of Lupus's torch their eyes gleamed gold.

"Flavia! Atticus!" said Jonathan without taking his eyes from the creatures. "Reach into my quiver and take out some arrows. Tear some strips from your handkerchiefs and wrap them around the tips. Quickly!"

Flavia's arrow was ready first. Jonathan let the arrow in his bow fall to the ground, and he nocked Flavia's instead. He pulled the bowstring back and then said, "Touch your torch to the tip of the arrow, Lupus!"

Lupus extended his torch, and when the flames ignited the scrap of cloth tied around its tip, Jonathan let go.

They saw the flaming arrow fly into the darkness.

"Yaaah!" crowed Lupus in triumph, and Flavia shrieked, "Yes! You got one! He's on fire!"

The flaming hyena ran off, and now the rest of the pack scattered with whoops of terror.

"We should go back by fire," said Nubia, gripping Jonathan's arm. "They must be very hungry to approach so close to people. They are wanting to eat the mules."

"Nubia's right," said Atticus. "We'll build up the fire into a proper blaze and bring the mules over."

"Yes," said Jonathan. "Good idea." His own voice sounded calm, but it was several moments before he could convince his trembling legs to turn and follow the others.

They left their camp before dawn, walking the mules by torchlight beneath a vibrant blue-black sky. By the time it was light enough to douse their torches, they had walked out the stiffness in their limbs and could mount the mules.

It was a mild gray morning, and the fields on either side of the road smelled of damp wicker and chamomile. They reached Eleusis midmorning and found the Sacred Way so crowded with pedestrians, carts, and wagons that they had to dismount again and walk. Atticus said it must be a market day in Athens.

They stopped twice, once to lay offerings at a shrine of Hermes, and once during a rain shower to finish the last of their olives and bread in the shelter of a mulberry tree. The rain did not last and by early afternoon the sun reappeared, making their cloaks and tunics steam. In the dripping trees on either side of the road sodden birds were beginning to twitter and purr.

Suddenly Flavia gasped and pointed straight ahead and turned to Atticus. "Look!" she cried. "I think I can see the Acropolis in the distance!"

He smiled and nodded at her, and she saw that the old sailor had tears in his eyes. "Yes," he said. "That's my Athens."

As they neared Athens, tombs began to appear by the side of the road, modest at first, then becoming grander as they neared the city. Many were marble, and Nubia could tell by the faded paint on some that they were very old. She caught a whiff of smoke from a foundry and also the smell of wet clay. There must be potteries nearby. One tomb caught her eye, and she turned her head to look at the carved relief of a little girl saying good-bye to her pet dog. The dog was painted black, and he reminded Nubia of her own puppy, Nipur, who was in Ostia. Tears filled her eyes and blurred her vision, so that she almost didn't see the man waving at her from behind the marble relief of a horse and rider.

Aristo. The man behind the grave marker was Aristo.

SCROLL XIX

Nubia's heart stuttered at the sight of Aristo beckoning her from behind a funeral stele. She looked around to see if any of the others had noticed. They hadn't.

Nubia touched Flavia's shoulder. "I am just going in bushes behind tombs for a moment," she said. "Take Piper's bridle. Don't wait for me. I will run fast to catch you."

"All right," said Flavia. "Don't be long."

Nubia let the mules pass by, then turned and wove her way back between other travelers to reach the side of the road. Aristo was there behind the marble slab. Without any greeting or explanation, he gripped her shoulders.

"Where is he?" he said. Up close in the bright morning light, she saw that he was thinner and that he had not shaved recently. "I've spent all morning trying to find him."

"Who?" asked Nubia.

"Dion, of course! My brother." He frowned at her and she frowned back. She didn't understand what he was asking.

"All I know," said Nubia, "is that Flavia thinks *you* are going to Temple of the Maiden and Cave of the Kindly Ones."

"Temple of the Maiden and Cave—why does she think that?"

"That is what the Pythia said."

"Of course! The Temple of the Maiden! Thank you!" He gave

her a quick kiss on the forehead and released his grip on her shoulders. "Now hurry back," he said, "before they suspect something. And Nubia!" She looked over her shoulder at him. "Try to slow them down for an hour or two. Just long enough for me to catch him."

Nubia nodded, then ran quickly through the pedestrians and around a flock of sheep. Where were her friends? Finally, she saw Atticus's gray hair up ahead and the mules' pointed ears.

"Nubia! Are you all right?" said Flavia. "You look strange."

"I am fine," Nubia stammered. "My stomach is a little unhappy."

"Do you want us to stop and wait while you go in the bushes again?"

"No, I am better now."

She walked in a daze, still feeling the heat where his lips had touched her forehead, and her shoulders, where he had gripped them. Why had he asked her about Dion?

By now the city walls had risen up, and the Acropolis had dropped out of sight. They approached a massive fortified gate—still bearing the scars of some ancient battle—and their pace slowed even more as the crowds funneled through. Nubia glanced at Flavia. She wanted to tell her what Aristo had said, but that would be a betrayal. She felt dizzy.

"Let's go this way," said Atticus. "A friend of mine used to own stables just outside the city walls. We can give the mules a rest. They'll just hold us up in this crowd. Agreed, Miss Flavia?"

"Agreed," said Flavia grimly. "We don't want anything to stop us now."

"Athens," whispered Flavia. "I can't believe I'm really here." She gazed around at tombs and workshops on either side of the road, and at houses and temples up ahead. Some buildings were of white marble, others red brick, like at Ostia. All of them had been scoured clean by the recent rain and gleamed in the late afternoon sun. "I thought it would be bigger," she murmured. "There are more trees and open spaces than I imagined."

"Most of the open spaces are markets," said Atticus. "See the colored awnings of the stalls? Those are mostly potters' stalls; we're near the Inner Ceramicus."

But Flavia was gazing up at the Acropolis. Like the Acrocorinth, it was a little mountain rising up in the middle of a plain. Unlike the Acrocorinth, its top was perfectly flat, as if a giant had sliced it off with an enormous knife. Temples gleamed like jewels on this level surface, and rising taller than any of them was the bronze statue of Athena, wearing her helmet and holding her spear.

"It's beautiful," she breathed.

"The Acropolis never disappoints," said Atticus.

"That temple there," said Flavia, pointing, "the one with the strange white roof and the blue squares above white columns. That's the Parthenon, isn't it, the Temple of the Maiden?"

"Yes," said Atticus. "That's Athena's temple."

"Then that's where he'll be," said Flavia. "Let's finish this."

"Behold!" cried Nubia suddenly, pointing toward a honey-colored temple on a green hill to their right. "Behold, I see Aristo!"

"Where?" cried Flavia. "Where is he?"

"There!" cried Nubia. "Follow me!" She began to run toward the temple. Tigris followed, barking, and Flavia ran after them.

"Where is he?" Flavia cried. She could hear the footsteps of the others behind her and the rhythmic rattling of Jonathan's arrows in their quiver.

"Up ahead!" said Nubia over her shoulder. "Wearing red cloak."

"I think I see him!" wheezed Jonathan. "Over there by that statue of Athena."

"Pollux!" gasped Flavia, breathing hard. "We must have lost him. . . . Can't see him anywhere. . . . Where are we, anyway?" She looked up at a long stoa with painted blue columns and a red-tiled roof.

"Agora," wheezed Jonathan. He was bent over, resting his hands on his knees, trying to catch his breath. "I think this is the . . . the main agora."

Lupus nodded; despite his limp he had been able to keep up with them.

"What is agora?" asked Nubia

"It just means a forum," said Megara. She was still dressed in her oversized boy's tunic, and there was a sheen of sweat on her pretty face. "I think one of the Academies is somewhere around here," she added.

"Where did he get to?" muttered Flavia. "I can't see him with all these people walking around."

"Oh!" cried Nubia. "Look at those strange men!"

Flavia impatiently turned to see a group of men strolling in the shade of the stoa. They all had long hair, short brown capes, and sandals laced up to their knees.

"They're Pythagoreans," said Megara. "Philosophers. We have some in Corinth." She pointed toward a large fountain house. "Those men with the short hair and smooth cheeks are Epicureans."

"Of course!" Jonathan had his herb pouch to his nose. "The famous philosophers . . . of Athens . . . and the men . . . with short beards . . . must be Stoics. They look just like . . . fresco of Seneca . . . at gladiator school."

"Where *is* he?" muttered Flavia, turning on the spot.

"You attended gladiator school?" said Megara to Jonathan.

Jonathan nodded.

"Who are those?" said Nubia. "The ones with the matty beards walking in the sun."

"I think those are Cynics," said Megara.

"Oh, Pollux!" cursed Flavia. "I can't see him anywhere. Nubia, are you certain it was Aristo you saw?"

Nubia nodded at Flavia and turned back to Jonathan. "What is a philosopher?"

"It means 'lover of wisdom,'" said Megara.

"Of course!" said Jonathan, lowering his herb pouch. "I just realized why they call them Stoics—because they walk around in the stoas. I think we lost him, Flavia."

"Philosophers discuss life and politics and ideas," said Megara to Nubia. "Their appearance often shows which philosophy they follow."

"Stop taking about philosophers!" cried Flavia. "We're here to catch Aristo."

Nubia ignored Flavia. "Which philosophers wear no clothings at all?" she asked, pointing.

They all turned to look, and Flavia squealed, "Great Juno's peacock! Those men over there are completely naked! Don't point, Nubia! Don't even look!"

But like the others, she couldn't take her eyes from the group of muscular and naked young men walking and laughing in the slanting sunshine.

"I don't think they're philosophers," said Megara. "They're probably just on their way to the gymnasium or the baths. We Greeks . . ." she trailed off.

"We Greeks what?" said Jonathan.

"Um . . . we Greeks aren't embarrassed by nudity," Megara was still staring wide-eyed at the young men. "It's completely natural," she murmured.

"Well, put your eyes back in your head," said Jonathan. "Here comes some more naturalness."

They all turned and followed his gaze to see a group of naked street urchins running toward them.

"Oh!" squealed Flavia and Nubia together. They both covered their eyes as three naked boys ran right up to them and held out their grubby hands. Tigris sniffed the boys' feet with interest, his tail going back and forth.

Megara spoke sharply to the beggars in Greek, and the two

youngest scampered off. But the third one wouldn't be budged. He was about eight years old and stood with his arms folded across his bare chest, glaring defiantly at them. He said something to Megara, who looked surprised, then laughed.

"He says he only costs one copper a day, and that he knows Athens better than anyone alive. He says he'll be our guide."

Flavia shook her head. "Tell him we don't need a guide. We have a native Athenian with us."

"Um, Flavia?" said Jonathan. "I think we've lost our native Athenian."

"What?"

"Atticus," said Jonathan. "I just realized he's not here. We must have lost him somewhere during the last part of that bracing run."

"Oh, Pollux!" cried Flavia. "Double Pollux!" She looked around the crowded agora. "Here we are stuck in the middle of a strange city without our bodyguard and guide. . . ." She took a deep breath and looked at the beggar boy. "Lupus, show him the portrait of Aristo." In halting Greek she said, "Have you seen this man?"

The boy peered at the painting on Lupus's tablet, then said in Latin. "Yes! I know. I am knowing this man!"

Flavia narrowed her eyes at him. "Are you sure?"

"I see him few minutes ago. I take you to him."

"All right," she said, and then turned to look up at the sky. "Megara, tell him to put on a tunic."

Megara and the boy exchanged words.

"He says he doesn't own a tunic."

"Oh for—" said Flavia, turning back. "Lupus, give him your old tunic, you know . . . the green one. I'll buy you a new one later. That green one's getting too small for you, anyway."

Lupus pursed his lips, then nodded as if to say: That sounds like a fair deal. He took off his knapsack, rooted around in it, and finally pulled out a crumpled olive-green tunic.

The boy's scowl dissolved into a look of bewildered joy as Lupus tossed him the garment. He slipped on the tunic and then reached for the woven belt Lupus was holding out. After tying the tunic at the waist, the boy shortened the hem by making it blouse up above the belt. Then he slowly looked up at them, apprehension on his face, as if he feared it was a cruel joke.

Their faces must have told him they were sincere, for he whooped with joy and punched both fists toward heaven. "Thank you!" he said in Greek, grasping Flavia's hand and fervently kissing it.

"Are people really so poor here?" she murmured.

"It looks like it," said Megara. "I suppose Athens wouldn't have been the best place for Nikos the beggar boy after all."

Before them, the little Athenian was spinning around, admiring his tunic and fingering his belt.

"Well, if he's going to be our guide," said Flavia with a sigh, "I suppose we'd better find out his name." She turned to the boy and said in Greek, "My name is Flavia Gemina, daughter of Marcus Flavius Geminus, sea captain. My friends are Nubia, Jonathan, Lupus, and Megara. And that's Tigris. What's your name?"

"Socrates," said the boy with a large grin.

They all laughed again, and Jonathan said, "Well, at least we know this beggar's not a girl in disguise."

Megara glared at him, then laughed. "I suppose I had that coming," she said.

SCROLL XX

Socrates the beggar boy led Flavia and her friends through the streets of Athens. They hurried along the street of metalworkers—suitably close to the Temple of Hephaestus—past a sanctuary of Aphrodite and several bronze statues toward another large stoa. Here Flavia could see dramatic paintings on the long wall behind the columns. She recognized Theseus fighting the Amazons, but another exciting battle did not look familiar.

"Painted Stoa," said Megara over her shoulder. "Socrates says it's the Painted Stoa."

Flavia forced herself to keep going. She longed to stop and look at these fascinating pictures. She longed to examine the statues of her favorite characters from Greek mythology. She longed to browse in bookshops like the one with the names of famous authors engraved in its marble doorposts. But she couldn't. She had to catch Aristo, if she was to save her father. With every passing hour it might be too late.

Now Socrates was leading them up past more market stalls. One stall sold spring flowers, another slabs of pungent, sweating cheese, still another specialized in jars of Hymettan honey. She saw loops of sausages, secondhand water clocks, twittering birds in cages, parchment scrolls, votive objects, dried fruit, and colorful cones of powdered spices, measured out on the gleaming bronze pans of scales. Some stall-keepers were beginning to pack away their goods, for it was approaching sunset.

They were climbing toward the Acropolis now. As she scanned the crowds for the flash of Aristo's red cloak, she suddenly noticed the other two beggar boys following them. So did Socrates. He drove them off with a torrent of abuse, supported by vigorous hand gestures and Tigris's barks.

"You know," whispered Jonathan to Flavia, "Socrates reminds me of someone."

They both looked back at Lupus, who was lingering by a stall that sold knives and axes. Lupus wore a sea-green tunic and good sandals. He had lightly oiled his dark hair and combed it neatly back from his forehead. "Just think of how much he's changed since we first saw him up that pine tree in Ostia," said Flavia. "Remember how savage and grubby he was?"

Jonathan grinned. "Remember the nits in his hair?"

"And how he thought our bottom-wiper was a drumstick?"

"He's changed a lot," said Jonathan, suddenly serious. "Grown up a lot."

"So have you," said Flavia.

Jonathan shrugged. "You're pretty much the same," he re-marked. "Always wanting to solve the problem. Always believing there's a solution. . . ."

"I'm not doing very well at catching Aristo or solving this mys-tery," she sighed.

"I think I know why," said Jonathan, wheezing a little as the road grew steeper. "Why you haven't solved it, I mean."

"Yes?" said Flavia.

"Because you're too emotional about it."

"What do you mean?"

"You love your father—"

"Of course I love him!" cried Flavia. "Every time I close my

144

eyes or try to sleep, all I can see is Pater lying there on that bed so pale and still. . . ."

"That's exactly what I mean. I think if someone else had been lying on that bed, you would have figured out why it happened by now."

Silence.

"Don't jump on me," said Jonathan, "but Nubia's had a good idea which she's afraid to tell you."

"What?"

"She thinks your father and Aristo switched rooms for some reason and that your father wasn't the intended victim."

"That's ridiculous! Of course Pater was the intended victim!"

"Why?" Jonathan stopped walking and turned to face Flavia. "Just because he's the center of your world doesn't mean he's the center of everybody else's world. He's not the omphalos."

The others had stopped, even Socrates the beggar boy. Tigris whined, then wagged his tail.

"How can you say such a thing?" cried Flavia. "Pater is lying at the Gates of Hades, unable to remember anything because he's been cursed as well as stabbed—"

"That's exactly what I'm talking about," said Jonathan. "You're too emotionally involved. Flavia, listen to me! Why would someone curse a man they're about to murder?"

Flavia stared at Jonathan. "I told you. Aristo decided to curse Pater and then changed his mind."

"No, it doesn't make sense. The other facts don't make sense either. You need to step back from this problem." He took a deep breath and spoke in a normal tone of voice. "Flavia, you need to 'know yourself,' as it says on the temple in Delphi."

"And be a cold block of marble like you?" said Flavia. "Someone who refuses to feel anything? No thank you."

"I'm not a block of marble!" shouted Jonathan. "And I'm not your slave for you to order around. I'm your friend. I've been try-

145

ing to help you. But if you won't even listen to me . . . Come on, Tigris!" he said. "We're leaving."

Flavia stared after him.

"Go, then! We don't need you, anyway!" She turned to the others. "Come on! Let's get on with it."

"Where's that boy taking us?" grumbled Flavia. "I saw the Acropolis above the roofs a moment ago. It's back that way."

"Don't worry," said Megara. "I'm sure he knows what he's doing."

"I'm not." Flavia still felt sick about Jonathan's decision to desert her.

A moment later Socrates led them around the corner and up a narrow street of shops. He stopped in front of one that specialized in baskets, mats, and bead curtains.

"Here we are," said Socrates. "Yes, please."

"Aristo's in here?" said Flavia. She was breathing hard because the street was on a slope.

"No," said Socrates. "My father is in there. This is shop of my father. He sell very cheap baskets. You buy some, please?"

Flavia took a deep breath and stepped toward Socrates. "If you don't show us the quickest way to the Acropolis," she said through gritted teeth, "I'll rip that tunic into a thousand pieces!"

"I am taking! I am taking!" He grasped her hand and pulled her farther up the hill past other shops, then out into a wider street with a vista over all of Athens. Socrates tapped her shoulder and pointed, and she turned to see the Acropolis looming above them, blotting out half the sky.

Flavia could see people up there looking down over a retaining wall. Behind the tiny faces were the roofs and colored columns of the temples, and behind the white roof of one temple rose the massive bronze head and shoulders of Athena, looking out over her city.

Lupus gave a low whistle.

"That Athena's even bigger than the Apollo at Delphi," breathed Megara, then turned to Socrates, who was talking to her. "He says this is the processional way. You can follow this road straight back down through the agora to the Dipylon Gate and on to Eleusis."

"I wish I'd known that earlier," muttered Flavia, and glared at Socrates.

As they walked up the steep road, the boy pointed to a green hill on their right. Its summit was a jumble of smooth, bone-colored boulders. Small shrines and pine trees dotted its grassy slopes.

"He says that's the Areopagus," translated Megara. "Beyond it is a hill called the Pnyx, where the assembly meets."

"The Areopagus!" cried Flavia. "Ask him if the Cave of the Kindly Ones is on the Areopagus?"

"Yes, he says there is a small sanctuary dedicated to the Kindly Ones, and you can see the cave mouth there, between those pine trees."

Flavia stopped walking. "If Aristo follows the Pythia's advice, then he'll go to the Parthenon first," she said. "But there's a chance he might already be at the Cave of the Kindly Ones. Lupus, will you and Socrates investigate while Nubia and Megara and I go up to the Acropolis?"

Lupus nodded, and Socrates bowed.

"Good. If you find him, then tell the priests or guards what he did and have them capture him. Then come find us. We'll be up at the Parthenon. Otherwise, let's meet at the base of the big Athena in half an hour. Oh please, Castor and Pollux, may we find him this time!"

Nubia followed Flavia and Megara up the steep hill toward the en-trance to the Acropolis. She heard a questioning "baaa?" behind her and saw two priests leading a lamb with a black and white face, presumably for the evening sacrifice. Other pilgrims were making their way up, including a few veiled women and one family. Some of them were also leading lambs or goats. One old man had a live rooster under one arm.

The approach funneled them through the huge marble columns of a monumental entrance whose roof was not of red tile but of white marble. Nubia mounted the smooth marble steps carefully, to avoid stepping on animal droppings. She also had to sidestep dozens of beggars who had positioned themselves here on the stairs. All were emaciated and half naked, and one man had no arms, just stumps that reached to where his elbows should have been. Nubia could not help staring, and she felt her throat tighten. How did the poor man eat or dress himself? And how had such a terrible thing happened?

A dozen more steps brought them to the highest level of the Acropolis.

"There are even more statues than at Delphi," said Nubia, gazing around.

"Probably about the same number," said Flavia. "They're just packed into a smaller area. Keep an eye out for Aristo. That must be the Parthenon straight ahead."

"It is beautiful," said Nubia, staring at the huge temple that rose above a forest of statues and altars. Massive white columns of fluted marble supported a gable full of colorful statues and an unusual white roof, like that of the entrance gate.

Her eye caught a flutter of red at the far end of this building, and her heart stuttered. Aristo! She had tried to get Flavia away from him, to give him the time he had asked for, but now here he was, as if by some prearranged appointment. She must act quickly.

"There he is!" cried Nubia, pointing toward a temple on her left with painted marble women instead of columns. "I saw Aristo go in there!"

"Where?" cried Megara.

"There!"

Flavia turned to look at Nubia. "Are you sure?"

"I am sure." Nubia could not look Flavia in the eyes, so she turned her head toward the painted temple on the left and pointed again. "I saw Aristo go there."

"No, Nubia," said Flavia quietly. "You didn't see him go in there. I know because I just saw him going into the Parthenon. Come on. This time we're not letting him escape!"

SCROLL XXI

"Come on, Nubia." Flavia gripped Nubia's wrist and pulled her up the marble steps past the massive white columns. Megara followed.

At the entrance, Flavia turned. "Megara, he might try to run away and we don't have Atticus with us, so see if you can find a priest or a guard. Tell them what happened. And keep an eye open for Dion. If he shows up, he can help us catch Aristo."

She pulled Nubia through the huge doorway in the east side of the Parthenon, the end farthest from the entrance to the Acropolis. She couldn't immediately see a red cloak, so she allowed herself to gaze at the cult statue towering at the far end of the vast space. The gold and ivory Athena was breathtaking, forty feet tall and gleaming in the pearly light, which filtered through the translucent white roof tiles overhead.

It was nearly sunset, so there were only a few people in the temple, groups and individuals, moving along the high-ceilinged central corridor. Still no red cloak, but there was a kind of balcony on either side, and people were walking up there, too. Flavia couldn't see any red cloak on the upper gallery at Athena's end because the ranks of white fluted columns on either side seemed to make a solid wall. The columns only separated from one another as she began to move forward. Down here on the ground floor, bronze grilles between the columns blocked off the side aisles, which were packed with hundreds of precious gifts to the goddess. Flavia saw painted statues, marble altars, wooden chests, ceramic vases, musical instruments, garlands made of gold leaf and silver. She had never seen a temple so packed with booty. It was like one of the treasure houses at Delphi, but on a massive scale.

She felt Nubia twist in her grip, so she stopped and turned toward her former slave girl.

"Why did you lie to me, Nubia?" she said. "You've never lied to me before, have you?"

"No," said Nubia, lifting her chin. "I have never lied before."

"Then why now?" Out of the corner of her eye, Flavia could see Megara silhouetted in the bright doorway. "Why did you tell me Aristo was going to that other temple when you saw him come here."

"Because Aristo did not attack your father. He told me."

Flavia gasped. "He *told* you? When?"

"Last night. In the green rain."

Flavia stared. She felt as if Nubia had slapped her in the face. "You saw him last night and you didn't tell us?"

Nubia hung her head. "He said he just needed to find him, to find out why."

"He needs to find whom?"

"I am not sure but I think Dion."

"Why?"

"I don't know."

Flavia's mind was spinning like a piece of clay on a potter's wheel. She shook her head, then pulled Nubia toward the image of Athena.

In front of them stood a group of about twenty turbaned men, staring up at the cult statue and discussing it with expansive hand gestures. As they turned and started to move back toward the

151

entrance, Flavia saw that the colossal statue was reflected by a shallow pool of water at its base. There were one or two other suppliants there, including a kneeling man. He had his back to them, but Flavia could see he wore a white tunic and that his hair was the color of bronze. She heard Nubia's sharp intake of breath.

The kneeling man was not wearing his red cloak but she knew immediately that it was Aristo. She had caught up with him at last.

Flavia looked around. There was no altar here for him to cling to so he could not seek sanctuary. She would ask the priests to seize him and deliver him to the authorities. Here in the House of the Maiden he would finally face her, his accuser, just as the Pythia prophesied.

But she could not see a priest and the smell of incense was making her feel sick. Suddenly she heard a cry of alarm that echoed in the vast space above. A man in a red cloak had just appeared from behind the statue's massive base.

As the figure moved forward, splashing through the shallow pool toward them, she saw Aristo rise from his knees to his feet and she heard him cry out again in terror.

The man coming toward him was himself.

For a moment, Flavia's mind was as blank as a freshly pumiced piece of parchment. How could Aristo be confronting himself?

Then the Aristo who had been kneeling turned and ran, and Flavia saw at once that he was not Aristo. He was taller and thinner and his hair frizzy rather than curly. The turbaned men scattered before him, and as he blundered within arm's length of Flavia she saw the terror in his eyes and caught an acrid whiff of sweat mixed with fear.

The man with the red cloak—the real Aristo—was running through the shallow pool now, his feet shattering the reflected image of the goddess. Someone shouted in Greek, and a few of the turbaned men turned to intercept him. Aristo knocked them aside. As he charged toward Flavia and Nubia his eyes did not even flicker their way. All his concentration was focused on the man he was pursuing, his brother Dion.

"Stop him!" someone was shouting in Greek. "Stop him!"

Aristo was within arm's length of them when suddenly Flavia saw Megara step forward. Aristo went flying headlong, sliding along the polished floor of the temple.

"Run, Dion! Run!" screamed Megara, scrambling to her feet. Aristo was on his feet, too. He shot Megara a furious look. Then he was off again, running fast, arms pumping, red cloak flapping. Megara started to run after them, but Nubia caught her arm.

"No!" cried Nubia fiercely, swinging Megara around and flinging her back down onto the marble floor. "Leave him alone!" Then she was off, running toward the bright doorway after Aristo and his brother.

Flavia stared, then followed Nubia through the huge doorway, between the massive columns, down the marble steps toward the round temple of Rome and Augustus. She heard screams and turned to see the crowds on her left part to make way for the running men.

She ran down the steps and turned to keep up with Nubia, who had doubled back and was weaving in and out of statues and steles, heading back toward the entrance of the Acropolis.

Flavia passed startled faces on her left and right, and almost tripped over a bleating lamb, but she regained her balance in time to see Lupus waiting at the base of the colossal Athena.

"Where are they?" she cried, when she reached him. "Which way have they gone?" She skidded to a stop on the marble path.

"Unnggh!" grunted Lupus and pointed toward the entrance of the Acropolis.

Flavia turned just in time to see Nubia's dark head disappearing among the crowds by the monumental entrance gate. But Nubia did not go through the gate and down the ramp. Instead she veered left again and disappeared between the elegant Ionic columns of a small temple.

"Come on, Lupus!" cried Flavia, and a few moments later they stood panting before a marble slab near the little temple. The altar was still dripping with blood from the evening sacrifice, and a dark plume of smoke rose up from it. The priest who had performed the ritual stood to one side of the altar, his fingers buried in the glistening entrails of the animal. His head was lifted and turned toward the retaining wall of the Acropolis.

Flavia followed his gaze and saw Dion crouched on top of the wall. She knew that beyond this wall was a sheer drop of maybe a hundred feet or more onto jagged rocks. Between the altar and the parapet, Aristo stood panting, his knife in his hand. Nubia stood a few paces behind him. Dion was muttering in Greek, both hands up, his eyes full of fear.

For a moment, the two brothers formed a strange frozen tableau against the pink backdrop of the evening sky.

Suddenly Flavia understood the Greek words Dion was repeating: "Forgive me! Forgive me!" His eyes were red and swollen with weeping.

Aristo shook his head and advanced toward his brother.

Dion glanced over the side and then—without a sound—he jumped.

As Dion leaped from the Acropolis, a woman screamed. Flavia turned to see Megara slump to the ground in a faint.

"Don't bother with her!" Flavia shouted to the priest. "Stop that man in the red cloak! He's a murderer! Get him!"

Then she gasped as Aristo heaved himself up onto the wall and disappeared over the side, too.

Nubia was at the parapet now, and Flavia ran to join her. She looked down, expecting to see two broken bodies on the rocks far below. But at this part of the wall, there was only a six-foot

154

scramble over slippery boulders past a roofed sanctuary built into the rock, and down to a path. The path forked left to a huge theater and right toward the Areopagus. The red light of the setting sun made the tall cypress trees throw long purple shadows across the rocky ground so that at first she could not see Aristo or his brother.

Then she saw the two running men: Aristo and his long shadow pursuing his brother down the path toward the right, toward the Areopagus.

Suddenly Nubia was on the wall beside Flavia.

"Nubia!" cried Flavia. "What are you doing? He'll kill you, too!"

But Nubia had already jumped down and was scrambling over pale boulders to the path. Now Lupus was on the parapet, too.

"No, Lupus!" cried Flavia. "You can't run with your bad ankle!" She looked back at the priest, who was fanning Megara with his hand. "Tell them what happened. Tell him to get help!"

Lupus only hesitated for a moment. Then he nodded and eased himself back off the parapet. "I'd better save Nubia," said Flavia, clambering ungracefully onto the parapet. "Wish me luck!"

Lupus gave her a thumbs-up.

Flavia sent up a silent prayer to Castor and Pollux. Then she jumped.

As Nubia ran down the slope of the Acropolis, she was intensely aware of everything around her: the sound of someone's sandals slapping on the path behind her, a bird's dusk warning cry, the tang of wood smoke and roasting meat from the evening sacrifices, and the two men running down the shadow-striped hill before her.

Dion was making straight for a green hill with a jumble of smooth boulders and painted shrines. Aristo was not far behind him. There were pine trees down there, and the recent rain had brought out lush green grass. She saw Dion disappear around the far side of the hill.

She heard her own breath as she rounded a pine tree on the steep incline of the slope. Then she saw the smooth marble wall of a sanctuary and beyond it the top of a cave in the craggy rock face. She remembered the prophecy: "He will receive the verdict in the Cave of the Kindly Ones." She wasn't sure what a verdict was, but she knew this must be the cave.

Although it was sunset, the barred bronze doors of the sanctuary gate were still open. Through its arch, Nubia could see that Dion had fallen on his knees before a statue of a woman. He was sobbing uncontrollably and talking to the statue in Greek.

Then he turned, and his eyes widened again and he ran. A tree blocked Nubia's view for a moment, but as she moved into the sanctuary she saw Aristo pausing before the statue of the woman, too, then moving off after Dion.

Nubia glanced around for help, but the sanctuary seemed deserted. There appeared to be no cult temple. There was only the cave, like a silently screaming mouth in the face of the rocky hill.

Nubia ran toward the cave mouth and then stopped to look at the painted marble statue that Dion had worshiped. The statue depicted a woman wearing a short fluttering tunic and holding a bronze torch that flickered with real flames, thin and pale in the pink light of dusk. Up close, Nubia could see that the Fury was beautiful, with large eyes, smooth skin, and parted lips. There were no snakes in her hair and none crawling on her arms.

Nubia remembered something Atticus had told them about the sanctuary of the Furies: *Anyone who enters will go out of their mind with terror.* Then she knew where the snakes would be. She turned and stepped toward the cave entrance. There, as she had expected, writhed a dozen snakes, eyes bright as rubies and forked tongues tasting the evening air.

If she wanted to help Aristo, she would have to follow him into that cave full of snakes and madness and terror and death.

"Stop, Nubia!" she heard Flavia gasp behind her. "Don't go in there! That's the Cave of the Kindly Ones. You'll go mad in there!"

"But I must," whispered Nubia to herself. "I must."

Flavia cursed as she saw Nubia disappear into the black mouth of the cave. Then she took a deep breath and stepped forward.

"Oh!" she squealed, as the last of the snakes poured themselves down into a small pit at one side. She stood with her hand pressed against her chest and murmured a quick prayer to Castor and Pollux, and to Athena, whose beautiful wise image was still clear in her mind.

The prayer seemed to help. The blood no longer roared in her ears and now she could hear shouts and cries deeper in the cave. She put out her hand to steady herself and her fingertips encountered stone, cool and smooth.

Rounding a curve in the narrow corridor she saw Nubia standing in the doorway of a cylindrical room. It was shaped like the inside of a leather scroll case, with a high, circular ceiling, a curving wall, and torches flaming in wall brackets. Flavia came closer and saw that at the center of this room stood a cube of marble. It was an altar, still bloody from an earlier sacrifice. Circling this altar—half-crouched and with their eyes fixed on each other—were Aristo and Dion.

Dion was weeping and repeating a phrase and even though he spoke in Greek Flavia understood him. "Forgive me, brother," he was saying. "I didn't mean to kill you."

With that one phrase—*I didn't mean to kill you*—all the pieces of the mosaic suddenly fell together in Flavia's mind: Dion's panic, Aristo's anger, the red leather sandals, the cloak, the knife, Tryphosa and Megara, even the rustling bushes on the night of their last dinner in Cenchrea. Flavia understood what must have happened the night her father was stabbed.

The revelation made her gasp. The answer had been there all along, as clear as a painted fresco on the wall. She had been so blind. So had the rest of them. Only Nubia had sensed the truth, and Megara, who had all the facts.

Dion was muttering to himself in Greek, his voice hoarse from screaming, tears running down his face, his arms extended as if to ward off something terrible.

"Be quiet!" Flavia shouted in Latin and was surprised by the sound of authority in her voice.

The brothers stopped circling each other and turned their heads to look at her.

"I don't know what he's babbling about," Aristo said to Flavia. "But I didn't do it. He did it. Nubia believes me, don't you?"

Nubia nodded.

"So do I," said Flavia. "But neither of you—be quiet, Dion!" She took a deep breath. "You each think you know what happened, but you're both wrong. Nobody here knows the whole truth." As Flavia squeezed past Nubia, she took her friend's hand and pulled her into the cylindrical room. Then she shut the heavy bronze door behind her and heard the bolt fall emphatically outside. "Nobody knows the whole truth," she repeated, "and we're not leaving here until we've found it."

SCROLL XXII

"Flavia, you fool, you've locked us in!" snapped Aristo.

"Hello, Aristo. It's nice to see you, too. I'm sure the priests will open the door at dawn," she said. "Or even sooner. Until then, sit down! And give me that knife." She stepped confidently forward, her hand extended.

He extended the knife handle first, and she took it with a silent prayer of thanks. It was a crude wooden-handled shepherd's knife.

Flavia tried to keep her voice steady. "Where's your other knife?" she asked him. "The one with the boar's-head handle?"

"At my parents' house in Corinth," he said. "Along with the rest of my things." Dion was still sobbing to himself in Greek.

"Speak Latin!" commanded Flavia, then glanced at Aristo. "I have a good Greek teacher but I'm still not fluent. And sit down! Sit on the bench and listen! You, too, Aristo." Dion and Aristo obediently sat on semicircular marble benches opposite each other.

"So," she said to Dion, "you killed Aristo. Your own brother."

"I didn't mean to," he sobbed. "By the gods I never meant to kill him."

"Your brother isn't dead. He's alive. Look!" Flavia thumped Aristo hard.

"Ow!" Aristo scowled up at her, rubbing his shoulder.

"See?" she said to Dion. "He's flesh and blood."

Dion stared. "Then you're not a ghost? I didn't kill you?"

"No, you blind fool!" Aristo's voice was cold with fury. "It wasn't me in that bed."

"Shhh!" said Flavia to Aristo, and to Dion: "How many fingers am I holding up?"

Dion blinked through his tears. "Three," he said.

Flavia moved closer to him, "And now?"

"Three? No, four. I mean . . ."

"You can't see things up close very well, can you?"

Dion hung his head. "No," he said. "I've had it from birth. Unlike him! He was perfect. Perfect sight, perfect hearing, perfect pitch, perfect looks . . ."

"You blind idiot!" said Aristo. "You didn't kill me. You killed my employer! My friend." His voice broke. "This poor girl's father."

"He's not dead, Aristo," said Flavia. "He survived."

Aristo turned wondering eyes on Flavia. "What? Not dead? But I'm sure . . . when I found him he was so still. There was so much blood!"

"Pater is alive," said Flavia, taking a deep breath. "He's very ill, but he's alive."

"Thank the gods." Aristo rested his head in his hands. "Oh, thank the gods." His shoulders began to shake.

Nubia perched on the bench beside him and put her hand on his back.

Dion's voice cracked. "But the Kindly Ones were chasing me and—I don't understand. . . ."

"I think I know what happened." Flavia walked back toward the bronze door, tapping the flat of Aristo's knife blade thoughtfully against the palm of her left hand. She turned to face Dion.

"Three nights ago," she said, "around dusk, you followed Aristo from your parents' house in Corinth to the hospitium in Cenchrea—the one where we were staying. Isn't that right?"

"Yes. Megara told me he had gone to meet Tryphosa."

160

"That little vixen!" Aristo lifted his face, and Nubia removed her hand from his back. "I wasn't with Tryphosa that night."

"You weren't with Tryphosa *that* night," said Flavia to Aristo. "But you'd spent other nights with her, hadn't you?"

Aristo looked from Flavia to Dion, then hung his head and nodded.

"I knew it!" cried Dion, wiping his nose with his arm. "You stole her from me."

Aristo snorted. "I didn't steal her," he said. "She practically threw herself at me."

"Anyway," said Flavia to Dion, "you followed Aristo to the inn that night, didn't you?"

Dion nodded. "Megara came to our house that morning. She said Tryphosa loved *him* not me, and that she could prove it. She told me to follow him one evening and see where he went. So I followed him that very afternoon. Later, in the garden, I heard him say he wasn't going back to Rome. . . ."

"You were hiding in the bushes, weren't you?" said Flavia. "We almost caught you."

Dion nodded. "I waited until it was dark and then I crept into the hospitium. I had to see if she was with him—"

"Tryphosa, you mean."

"Yes. I started to pull back the curtains, looking for the room with the Orpheus fresco."

"Of course!" said Flavia. "You heard us talking about that, too."

"It was dark," said Dion, "but I could see the painting of Orpheus on the wall. And I could hear *him* breathing. He always used to keep me awake with his breathing. By Zeus, I hated that! And I could smell her perfume. Her scent was in the room."

"What scent does Tryphosa use?"

"Myrtle. Myrtle and rose oil."

"So you started to strangle him."

"No. It was dark, and I couldn't tell if there was one figure or

161

two in the bed, so I took a step closer and leaned over. Suddenly his fist came up. He hit me here," he pointed to his bruised left cheekbone. "That made me so angry. I took him by the neck and started to squeeze, and then he was squeezing my neck, too—see? See the marks?"

Flavia nodded. "Then what?"

"It was dark in the room, but suddenly it was getting even darker and I knew I was losing consciousness. So I let go of his neck and used my knife. I only used it until his grip loosened, but I knew I'd killed him." Dion began to sob.

"Luckily you didn't kill him," said Flavia coldly, then turned to Aristo. "You weren't in the Orpheus room, were you? You switched rooms with Pater for some reason," Flavia glanced at Nubia, but her friend's eyes were fixed on Aristo.

"Yes," said Aristo. "You could only reach his room through mine. Because he intended to leave before dawn he suggested giving me the inner room, so that he wouldn't disturb me when he left."

"Were you not going to come with us to the ship to say farewell?" said Nubia. "You promised you would."

Aristo looked at her and then away. "I don't know. I felt so bad. . . . I was so tired. Marcus and I had stayed up late talking."

"Did Pater agree to cancel your contract?" said Flavia.

"Of course," said Aristo. "Your father was very gracious. He always has been. That's why I felt so terrible when—" He shook his head. "Praise the gods he's alive."

Flavia nodded and turned back to Dion. "Do you understand what happened? You assumed it was Aristo in the bed, but it was really my father. He's older, but he's about the same height and build. Also," said Flavia, "he wears myrtle-scented oil."

"Dear gods!" whispered Dion. "I attacked the wrong man." He rose slowly and looked at Aristo. "I attacked the wrong man," he whispered. "I thought I killed you and that your ghost was pursuing me. I thought I was mad. But I saw them! I saw the Kindly Ones . . . hiding in the shadows, among the trees, behind columns in the moonlight. Once I even heard them laughing at me. They were everywhere and they wouldn't leave me alone."

"The Furies pursue the guilty," said Aristo in a tired voice. "You may not have killed me, but you wanted to."

"You wanted to kill me, too," said Dion, nodding toward the knife in Flavia's hand.

"Maybe." Aristo shrugged.

"Why did you decide not to go back to Rome?" said Dion, suddenly. "It's because of Tryphosa, isn't it?"

Aristo sighed and shook his head. "No, it's nothing to do with her."

Dion stood up and looked down at his brother. "I never complained when you went off on your travels, leaving me to look after Mother and Father. Even though all they talked about was you and how wonderful you were. I was glad to have you out of my life. This year, for the first time, things were going well. I found a woman I could marry. My business was prospering. Then you came back and ruined everything. Why won't you go away again?"

"Yes, Aristo," said Flavia. "Why didn't you want to come back to Ostia with us? Don't you like us anymore?"

"You know why," said Aristo wearily.

"Is it Miriam?" asked Nubia.

Aristo glanced at her. "Of course it is." He turned to look up at Dion. "You say I have everything, but I can't have the one thing I really want. I can't bear seeing her and not being able to be with her. Are you happy now?"

"You mean there's a woman somewhere on earth who doesn't love you?" asked Dion in mock amazement. He stared up at the dark ceiling. "Maybe the gods have heard my prayers after all!" He muttered something in Greek.

Aristo growled a reply in the same language, and then launched himself at Dion.

"Stop it, you two!" cried Flavia, as the brothers rolled on the stone floor. "Nobody's died yet, but someone might if you don't stop acting like children!"

Aristo thrust Dion angrily away and stood up. He was breathing heavily. Dion remained lying on his back, staring up at the soot-blackened ceiling.

"I'm sorry I tried to kill you, Aristo," he said presently. "I'm glad you're alive. So glad. Please will you forgive me?"

Aristo turned away.

Still lying on the floor, Dion began to weep again.

"Aristo," said Nubia quietly. "Look how much he suffers. His feet are bloody and he is so thin and pale. He is being tormented."

"My feet hurt, too," said Aristo. But he stretched out his hand, and when Dion grasped it he pulled his brother to his feet.

"Anyway, it's not *my* forgiveness you need to ask," said Aristo, and turned to Flavia. "It's hers."

Dion looked at Flavia. "I'm sorry I almost killed your father," he said. "Will you forgive me? If you do, then perhaps the Furies will leave me alone."

"No," said Flavia. "I won't forgive you. My father doesn't recognize me anymore. He can't even remember who he is. He may never get better. You did that to him, Dion, and I want justice!"

Flavia's outburst had obviously exhausted her, because now she slumped beside Nubia on the semicircular marble bench. The walls of the cylindrical room were covered with hundreds of votive plaques of silver, bronze, copper, and painted terra cotta. They glinted in the flickering torchlight.

Nubia looked from Dion to Aristo, then back. "Dion," she said softly, "why do you hate Aristo so much?"

Dion raised his head from his hands and looked at her in surprise. Then he gazed at his brother. "I didn't always hate Aristo," he said slowly. "When we were little, I used to think the sun rose and set on him. He was my wonderful older brother, the golden boy. But as I got older I realized I would never be as clever or musical as he was. Mother and Father claim to love us both equally, but their eyes never light up when I come into the room."

"That's not true," said Aristo. "They love you."

"You say that, but all they ever talk about is you," said Dion, bitterly. "When you first left Corinth I was so glad. I thought finally they'd begin to appreciate me. After all, I was the dutiful one. The one who stayed to look after them. But you're still the one they praise." He closed his eyes.

"Why did you leave Corinth, Aristo?" asked Flavia. "I mean the first time, the night you saved Pater's life? What was the argument that made you so angry?"

He shook his head. "I can't even remember now. We were always arguing, and one day he just said something and I thought, *this is too much.*"

"I remember what upset you," said Dion. "I remember it clearly because the day you left was the best day of my life. It was your lyre. I broke it."

"That's right!" said Aristo. "You broke my lyre right before a dinner party Father was giving."

"You can repair a lyre," said Dion. "But you can't repair a broken heart."

In the silence that followed, Nubia heard the crackle of the pinewood torches. The flames flickered, and it seemed to her that the light in the room was growing dimmer.

Dion looked at Flavia. "What are you going to do to me?" he asked.

"I'm going to take you back to Corinth," she said, "and if Pater's not well enough to take you to court, then I will."

"Wonderful," he sighed. "I've just confessed everything so

you'll have no trouble winning your case. You know what they'll do to me, don't you? If I'm lucky they'll send me to the mines. If not, they may execute me."

"Good," said Flavia, though she felt faintly nauseous.

"In either case I'll have to stay in Greece," sighed Aristo, "to look after Father and Mother."

"You were thinking maybe you would not stay in Greece but come back to Ostia after all?" said Nubia. Her voice sounded small and strange in the echoing room.

"Yes," said Aristo. "Over these past three days I've had plenty of time to think about things. Like the fact that I have a brother who hates me so much he tried to kill me."

"That reminds me, Aristo," said Flavia, pausing for a moment to yawn. "Why didn't you tell us that you were innocent? That Dion did it?"

"I didn't know Dion did it. At first I had no idea what was happening." Aristo leaned back against the wall, and some of the votive plaques clinked softly. "I'd fallen asleep, but some thumps from next door woke me. I was sleeping in my tunic, with my cloak as a blanket. I pulled it around me and ran into your father's room. It was very dim, but I was just in time to see a figure running out the door. All I could tell was that it was a man. Then I went closer to the bed and saw Marcus and the knife in his shoulder. When I pulled it out, I recognized the handle. I bought that knife myself, and gave it to Dion for his last birthday. I was too stunned to speak."

Aristo yawned and closed his eyes. "The slaves were dragging me toward the main road when a woman screamed somewhere in the darkness up ahead. One of the slaves ran off to investigate, and I seized the moment. I head-butted the one holding me. He collapsed like a big baby and dropped his torch. I ran away as fast as I could. There was just enough starlight for me to find the main road."

"You didn't kick him senseless?" said Flavia.

"Of course not," said Aristo with a look of surprise.

"That explains why he looked fine the next day," murmured Flavia. "But Helen said you had an accomplice, the woman who screamed."

"I have no idea who she was," said Aristo.

"I do," said Dion. "It was Nikostratos's daughter, Megara. I don't know what she was doing lurking in the shadows there. I almost ran into her, and when she saw me she screamed. There was blood on my tunic," he added, "and I suppose I looked half-mad; I thought I'd killed you."

"Did you speak to her?" asked Nubia.

"To Megara?" said Dion. "Why should I speak to her? I assumed she was keeping guard while Tryphosa was with him." He glared at Aristo.

"I told you," said Aristo, "Tryphosa wasn't with me that night."

"Not that night, then. But other nights."

Aristo shrugged and looked away.

"How could you go with Tryphosa, knowing I loved her?"

Aristo did not reply.

"Tell us about Tryphosa, Dion," said Nubia softly.

Dion turned to Nubia. "She's wonderful," he said. "She's not like any of the women I've ever met in Corinth. She's beautiful, and she has spirit and courage. I suppose she's more like you Roman girls. Most girls in Corinth gasp and swoon if you talk to them."

"Tryphosa is totally unsuitable for you, Dion," said Aristo. "She's vain and vapid, and she'll go with anyone."

"Anyone but me, apparently," said Dion with a hollow laugh. "You know, it would be funny," he added, "if it didn't hurt so much."

"You deserve someone better," said Aristo. "Someone who loves you."

"I'd settle for any girl who doesn't like you," said Dion with a yawn.

"Not much chance of that," said Aristo, straight-faced. Then he winked at Dion, and they both laughed.

"I know a girl who can't stand Aristo," said Flavia, with a quick glance at Nubia.

"Who?" said Dion, sitting up. "Tell me her name. I'll marry her tomorrow."

"Megara," said Flavia. "Your neighbor. The girl we've just been talking about."

"That little thing?" said Dion. "I suppose she's pretty enough, but she's so timid. Like all the other girls here in Achaea. Maybe I should look for a wife in Italia." He yawned again.

"I think you might be surprised the next time you see Megara," said Flavia. "She's not as timid as you think."

Nubia gripped Flavia's arm and squeezed it hard.

"Don't worry, Nubia," Flavia whispered in her friend's ear. "I won't say any more."

"It is not that," whispered Nubia. "It is the torches. They are dying."

"Then we can get some sleep," said Flavia with a yawn. "I'm feeling very tired and—"

"No, Flavia," said Nubia. "It is not the dark I am worrying for. I think we are running out of air!"

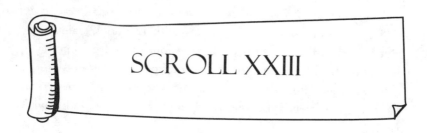

SCROLL XXIII

"It's no use," gasped Aristo after their third attempt to shoulder open the heavy bronze door. "There's probably a big oak bar on the other side. It must have fallen down when Flavia closed it. It's no good shouting any more. If there was anyone out there, they would have heard us."

Nubia gazed at Aristo. He was gleaming with sweat, and in the red light of the dying torches he looked like a statue made of Corinthian bronze.

"Aristo, the knife!" she said suddenly. "Can you stick knife in crack?"

"Yes!" cried Flavia. "You could slip it between the door and the wall and use it to push up the bolt!" She handed the knife to Aristo.

"Good idea!" he said, but a short time later he cursed and struck the door with his fist. "I can't even get it into the crack. The room is completely sealed."

"Why?" cried Flavia. "Why did they make it so dangerous?"

Aristo just shook his head. He was breathing hard.

"The priests probably won't be here until dawn." Dion sat panting beside his brother. "That must be hours away."

"I'm so sorry," cried Flavia. "It's all my fault. If only I hadn't closed the door. Now we're all going to die."

"Probably," said Dion. He was still breathing hard. "One little action . . . can lead to another . . . and before you know it . . . people are dying."

"I only meant to close the door," said Flavia in a small voice.

"I only meant to see if Aristo was with Tryphosa," said Dion. "But I nearly killed a man and now the four of us are all going to die. It only took one spark to set Troy on fire," he whispered.

It was very dim in the Cave of the Furies, and Nubia could barely see her friends. But she reached over and squeezed Flavia's hand.

"Oh, Nubia," whispered Flavia. "I'm so sorry I brought you here to Athens and that you're going to die. I've been so foolish. I should have listened to you and Jonathan and Lupus. Will you forgive me?"

"Yes," said Nubia, "I will forgive you. You have been a good friend to me and I love you."

"Oh, Nubia! I love you, too!"

The two girls hugged each other for a moment, and Nubia felt Flavia trembling.

"Aristo," said Dion, "I didn't mean to hurt you . . . or anyone. I only wanted my own place in the world."

"I know," said Aristo. "I'm sorry, too. I never knew how much you were hurting."

The two brothers looked at each other.

"Pax?" said Dion.

After a pause Aristo nodded. "Pax." Then he closed his eyes and slowly let his back slide down the polished bronze door until he was sitting on the ground.

Nubia felt sick and dizzy. She knew she was dying, but in her head music was playing. It was one of Aristo's songs. She gazed at him as he sat on the floor with his back against the door. His curly hair was tousled and his eyes were closed and his lips slightly parted. As the music filled her head she knew Aristo was the love of her life. Even if she had lived to be a hundred years old she would never have loved him any more than she did at this moment. He was panting lightly and she could see his chest rising and falling. They only had a few more breaths left in this life. If she was ever going to tell him how she felt, it must be now.

Nubia rose to her feet. She fought the dizziness that made the room spin around her and looked down at him.

"Aristo," she said, barely able to hear the words above the sound of the music in her heart. "Aristo, I have something to tell you, too."

The words were on Nubia's lips, but before she could say them Aristo fell backwards. The door had swung open behind him. The torches suddenly burned brighter and a cool wave of pine-scented air filled the cave.

The combined sense of relief and regret was so great that Nubia's world grew black for a moment. She found herself slumped awkwardly on the cool stone floor with a hot wet tongue lathering her face. Tigris! Then his tongue was gone, and she heard the clicking of his claws as he went to greet the others. The air was still full of swirling black spots and she couldn't see, so she took another deep drink of cool air, filling her lungs with it.

"Lupus!" she heard Flavia cry. "Jonathan! You came just in time. We were almost out of air!"

"How did you get in here?" said a man's angry voice. "This is sanctified ground. Explain your presence here."

As Nubia's vision finally cleared, she saw a scowling priest in black robes standing behind Jonathan and Lupus.

"The Kindly Ones led us here," said Dion, "and they have granted us mercy."

"Then your deaths would not have pleased them," said the priest, a little less harshly. "Tell me what happened."

Flavia began to speak, and Nubia saw amazement on the faces

171

of Jonathan, Lupus, and the priest as she explained what had happened. It took a long time to tell the whole story, because the priest kept asking for details.

"So no person here is tainted with a relative's blood?" he said at last.

"No one," they all said.

"Have you two reconciled?" he asked Aristo and Dion.

The brothers glanced at each other. Aristo shrugged, then nodded.

"And all is forgiven?"

"I'm not sure," said Dion, turning to Flavia. "Is all forgiven?"

Flavia dropped her gaze. She was so glad that they were alive and that she would see her father again, but Dion had done a terrible thing. How could she forgive him?

"Flavia," Nubia whispered in her ear. "If you forgive him, then Aristo will not have to stay with aged parents and he can come home with us."

Flavia looked at her friend's pleading eyes and remembered how Nubia had forgiven her a few hours before, when it seemed they must surely die. She nodded and turned to Dion.

"All right, Dion," she said. "I forgive you. I won't take you to court. But if my father chooses to do so, I won't stop him."

"That's all I ask," said Dion. "Thank you, Flavia Gemina. You are a wise maiden, almost as wise as Athena herself."

"Behold!" exclaimed Nubia, as they emerged blinking and squinting into brilliant light. "It is morning!"

There was something so pure about the bright spring morning with its golden sunshine and green leaves that Nubia felt the whole world was new. Birds sang, butterflies twinkled, and in the cool shade of a pine tree beside the sanctuary wall, a priest was pouring a crystal arc of water from a wooden bucket into a marble tank.

Nubia ran to the tank and cupped her hands and drank from it, not minding the Gorgons' snaky heads carved on its side. The others were suddenly beside her, drinking and laughing. Even Tigris lapped at the overflow on the ground.

Then Aristo plunged his whole head and shoulders in the tank and rose up with the water pouring off him like some river god. He had four days' growth of beard on his tanned cheeks, and Nubia had a sudden desire to reach up and touch it, to see if it would be rough or soft under her fingertips. He was smiling around at them, and for a moment his smile shone on her and it was like looking at the sun. She could not endure its brilliance and had to look away. As she turned, her eye caught a movement through the bronze bars of the sanctuary. A gray-haired man stood scowling in at them.

"Atticus!" she cried, and the others turned to look.

"Atticus!" cried Flavia. "Where were you?"

"Where was I?" he shouted, as the priest unlocked the gate and let him in. "The question is where were *you*? You frightened me to death running off like that. One moment you're beside me, the next you've vanished, apparently swallowed up by the earth, and I'm running around like a headless chicken! Are you up on the Acropolis? No, you're not. Are you on the Areopagus? No, you're not. So finally I go back to the stables and find Jonathan stalking up and down with a face as dark as Hades."

Jonathan grinned. "But we stopped being angry and started getting worried when you weren't back by sunset," he said. "Then Lupus came and explained what had happened."

"Jonathan insisted we get torches and set off to find you," said Atticus. "The Sanctuary of the Kindly Ones looked completely deserted, so we tried the Acropolis—and let me tell you, it's not easy to get into after dark. We searched for hours, but no sign of you there. So we came here. I helped these two over the wall and Tigris squeezed through the bars of the gate. Then nothing for hours! Oh, dear!" he added, mopping his nut-brown face with a cloth. "Life on dry land is too much for me. Who's for sailing back to Corinth today?"

Flavia stared at Atticus, and he grinned.

"I asked around yesterday," he said. "There's a ship that leaves for the Isthmus at noon. If we catch it and if the wind is fair we'll be in Cenchrea this evening. You can all come," he added, looking at Aristo and Dion. "The captain says there's plenty of room."

"Can we take mules?" asked Nubia.

"Yes, we can take the mules back to Helen."

"Oh, Atticus!" cried Flavia. "You're wonderful. That means we'll be with Pater tonight." She clapped her hands and jumped up and down.

Suddenly she stopped and looked at Nubia. "What about Megara?"

"She turned up at the stables, too," said Atticus. "She apologized for what she'd done."

"What did she do?"

"She was the one who cut the harness," said Atticus. "She said she only wanted to slow us up, not send us rolling over the precipice. Poor thing. I gave her a few coins and told her to go to the baths."

"Are you talking about little Megara?" said Dion. "Our next-door neighbor?"

Aristo nodded. "She tripped me up yesterday, just as I was about to catch you. She was trying to help you escape."

"Why would she do that?" asked Dion.

Flavia smiled. "You'll have to ask her that."

"Is there anywhere to have breakfast around here?" said Aristo. "My resurrection has given me quite an appetite. I'm absolutely ravenous."

"Mmmm," said Flavia, dipping her warm flat bread into the creamy white mixture in the black-glazed bowl. "This is like ambrosia."

174

"What is ambrosia?" asked Nubia.

"The food of the gods," laughed Flavia. "What's in this?"

"Yogurt, cucumber, dill weed, and garlic," said Atticus. "Lots and lots of garlic. Have you ever tasted anything so good?"

"Never," said Flavia. "This bread is wonderful, too."

The seven of them and Tigris were sitting at a table in the sunny colonnade in front of the Hydria Tavern, by the Tower of the Winds in the Roman Agora.

"Here, Tigris," said Jonathan. "Try some ambrosia on bread."

Tigris wolfed it down and wagged his tail.

"It feels as if I haven't eaten in days," said Dion, and pushed his empty plate away. "Excuse me, miss!" he cried into the tavern doorway. "Could you bring me another bowl of this? And some more bread?"

"Me, too!" said Aristo.

"Why not?" said Jonathan.

Lupus nodded enthusiastically, and Tigris barked.

A plump serving girl came out with a basket of bread and three bowls of garlic yogurt. Before she turned to go, she flashed Dion a dimpled smile.

"She liked the look of you, little brother," whispered Aristo as she disappeared back into the tavern. "See? You can easily attract a girl, a far better one than Tryphosa."

"I suppose Tryphosa is a bit of a tramp, isn't she?" said Dion, dipping a piece of warm flat bread in the yogurt mixture.

Aristo grinned and nodded. "Wait for the right girl, little brother," he said. "She'll come along."

At that moment Flavia saw a slender figure appear from behind a blue-painted column. The young woman was looking at Dion, and the eyes above her veil were beautiful, long-lashed, and dark. Dion stared back at her, his piece of bread poised between plate and mouth.

Flavia frowned. The woman's kohl-lined eyes looked familiar.

Tigris seemed to think so, too. He was sniffing her feet and wagging his tail. Then Flavia saw a beggar boy in a faded green tunic hopping up and down behind the woman, and she felt a grin spread across her face.

"Aristo's right," said the young woman to Dion. "Sometimes the right girl is right in front of you."

She pulled the veil from her face.

Dion's jaw dropped. "Megara?" he said. "Is that you?"

Flavia saw that Megara had been to the baths. Her skin was clean and pale, and her lips stained pink with some kind of berry juice. She looked beautiful.

Megara nodded and giggled. "Is there enough ambrosia for me?" she asked, squeezing onto the bench beside Dion. "I'm starving."

SCROLL XXIV

Three hours later—a little past noon—a ship named the *Nereid* set sail from Piraeus. It bore eight passengers, four mules, and one dog across the glittering blue Saronic Gulf toward the Isthmus of Corinth.

They docked in Cenchrea at sunset, and it was just growing dark when the four eager mules trotted up the familiar gravel drive of Helen's Hospitium toward their own stables. Syriacus looked up from lighting the torches on either side of the main doors, and when he saw them coming he hurried inside. By the time they had dismounted and reached the main entrance they saw Helen standing in the golden rectangle of the lighted doorway. She stood stiffly and twisted her hands together.

One look at her face confirmed Flavia's fears.

"I'm sorry, Miss," whispered the monkey-faced doctor Agaclytus. "I've done everything I can, but it's been nearly a week and he shows no sign of recovering his memory. He just sleeps and sleeps. I believe that with every day that passes, the chance of him remembering grows less. I am truly sorry."

Flavia stood looking down at her father. In the torchlight, his face looked pale and thin against the red embroidered cushion, and he was frowning in his sleep.

"Even in your dreams you look lost," whispered Flavia. She bent her head and heard the doctor's footsteps going quietly away. "Pater," she whispered, "I'm so sorry! I tried to find the person who cursed you so that I could stop the curse, but there was no curse, and now I don't know what to do! I don't know what to do to help you remember. I'm sorry, Pater. I'm so sorry."

Flavia suddenly recalled riding in a cart past Italian vineyards on a sunny morning, watching her father and his brother Gaius on horseback, laughing and talking together, looking like Castor and Pollux. That had been less than a year ago. The contrast between the image of his handsome laughing face in bright sunshine and the pale thin face in this dim room hurt her heart.

She felt as if she had cried a lifetime's worth of tears over the past week, but more were welling up behind her eyes and she was too tired to stop them. She cried and cried, and her tears fell hot and wet onto her father's sleeping face.

"Flavia?" Her father was looking up at her with reproach in his gray eyes.

"Flavia," he whispered. "Where have you been?"

"Oh, Pater!" cried Flavia. "You know who I am!"

He nodded, and Flavia hugged him gently, so she wouldn't hurt his wounds.

"I was having the worst nightmare," he said. "It was terrible. I dreamed I was wandering in a maze and couldn't find my way out."

"It's all right now, Pater," said Flavia. "You're out of the maze. You're going to be fine, and we're going to take you home to Ostia as soon as the doctor says you can travel."

Five days later, on the Ides of May, the *Delphina* set sail from Lechaeum for Ostia. Greece sank beneath the horizon at sunset while they dined on Atticus's chicken and chickpea stew. Later, when the stars pierced the dark blue canopy of the heavens, they sat on the polished bench beside the long table and prepared to play music.

Nubia was pretending to practice the fingering on her cherry-wood flute, but she was secretly watching Aristo from under her eyelashes. He was tuning Jonathan's barbiton.

"Oh, Flavia," said Jonathan. "I forgot to tell you something. I think the Pythia's prophecy for you might have been right after all."

Flavia looked at him and frowned. "*No man or woman has ever tried to kill your father,*" she recited, "*and no one ever will. Polydeuce's brother will live long and prosper. And he will regain his reason on the day it rains from a clear sky.*"

"See?" he said. "No man or woman ever tried to kill him. Dion tried to kill Aristo, not your father."

Flavia's eyes grew wide. "You're right, Jonathan! Also, Polydeuces is the Greek name for Pollux. Castor and Pollux are the Gemini, the Twins!" She pointed to the constellation, which hung above them in the night sky.

"And your father is the younger of two twins," said Aristo, glancing up from the ivory peg he was turning. They all looked toward Captain Geminus, who was swinging gently in the hammock they had strung between the deckhouse and mainmast. Without opening his eyes he raised a hand and waved at them.

"That's right," said Flavia, with a laugh. "As the younger twin, he's more like Castor than Pollux. He's like Polydeuces' brother, so that means he'll 'live long and prosper.' Oh, what a good prophecy! Did you hear that, Pater? You're going to live long and prosper! But I still don't understand the part about it raining from a clear sky. It wasn't raining the evening Pater regained his senses."

"Were you crying right before your father woke up?" asked Jonathan.

Flavia's gray eyes grew wide. "How did you know that?"

He grinned. "Apart from the fact that you'd been leaking like a

179

sieve all week? It was something I read in the guidebook, in the section about Delphi. There was a man who wanted something badly, I forget what. But the Pythia told him he would get it on the day it rained from a clear sky. Of course it never did rain from a clear sky. He got so depressed that he went home and laid his head in his wife's lap. It upset her to see him so sad and she started to weep for him and as her tears fell on his face, he suddenly realized that it was raining from a clear sky because her name was Aethra, which means 'clear sky.'"

"This feels true," said Nubia to Flavia. "I often think that your eyes are the color of the sky."

"Great Juno's peacock!" whispered Flavia. "You're right. The Pythia's prophecy came true. The god really did speak through her."

Aristo handed Jonathan his barbiton and took up his lyre. "Are we ready?" he asked. "Who wants music?"

"I do," came Captain Geminus's voice from the hammock, and they all laughed again.

Jonathan began to play, plucking notes so deep that Nubia felt rather than heard them. Flavia jingled her tambourine softly, and Lupus's drumming was as steady as a heartbeat, so that it was almost transparent. It was as if they were afraid to intrude on the sound of her flute as it entwined itself with the honeyed notes of Aristo's lyre. Soon their music filled the sails, the night, the world. It was like a heady perfume that made Nubia want to swoon.

It seemed to her that she and Aristo had never been so in tune with each other. But when she looked at him, utterly lost in his music, she suddenly realized that he was not thinking of her but of someone else. He had no idea how she felt about him. It was because he didn't know that he could abandon himself so completely to the music. If he ever found out how she felt, it might spoil their music, which was as important to her as air or food or water.

She knew then that she must keep her love for him hidden. It would be like a knife in her heart, twisting each time he spoke to her or smiled at her, but if that was the price to pay for moments like this, then she would endure it.

FINIS

ARISTO'S SCROLL

Academy (uh-**kad**-em-ee)
Greek word for the garden near Athens where Plato taught; other schools of philosophy and rhetoric later came to be called academies after it

Achaea (a-**key**-uh)
after Rome destroyed Corinth in 146 B.C., most of Greece became a Roman province known as Achaea, with rebuilt "Roman" Corinth as its capital (see map)

Acrocorinth (uh-**krok**-oh-rinth)
the dramatic mountain that rises above Corinth; it was the site of a sanctuary and the notorious temple of Aphrodite, attended by beautiful priestesses

acropolis (uh-**krohp**-oh-liss)
literally: "highest point of a town," usually the site of temples and sanctuaries and very often fortified; the most famous one was the Acropolis of Athens

Aegean (uh-**jee**-un)
sea between modern Greece and Turkey

Aegeus (aj-**ee**-uss)
mythological king of Athens and father of the hero Theseus

Aeneid (uh-**nee**-id)
> epic poem by the Roman poet Virgil about the Trojan hero Aeneas

Aeschylus (**ess**-kill-uss)
> Greek tragic poet who flourished in the fifth century B.C.; he wrote the *Eumenides*

Africus (**aff**-rick-uss)
> wind from the south (strictly, south southwest) which often brings stormy seas

Agamemnon (ag-uh-**mem**-non)
> king of Mycenae and leader of the Greeks who sailed to fight against Troy

agora (ah-gore-**ah**)
> Greek for "forum," or "marketplace"

Alexandria (al-ex-**and**-ree-ah)
> port of Egypt and one of the greatest cities of the ancient world

altar
> a flat-topped block, usually of stone, for making an offering to a god or goddess; often inscribed, they could be big (for temples) or small (for personal vows)

amphora (**am**-for-uh)
> large clay storage jar for holding wine, oil, or grain

Aphrodite (af-fro-**dye**-tee)
> Greek goddess of love; her Roman equivalent is Venus

Apollo (uh-**pol**-oh)
> god of the sun, music, and disease and healing; his special sanctuary was in Delphi

Areopagus (air-ee-**op**-a-guss)
> hill at the foot of the Acropolis in Athens; this is where Orestes received judgment for his crime, in Aeschylus's play the *Eumenides*

Artemis (**ar**-tem-iss)
Greek goddess of the hunt, known as Diana in the Roman world

Athena (ath-**ee**-nuh)
Greek name for Minerva, goddess of wisdom and war

Attica (at-ick-uh)
famous region of Greece; with Athens as its major city; part of Achaea in the first century A.D.

barbiton (**bar**-bi-ton)
a kind of Greek bass lyre; Jonathan's "Syrian" bass barbiton is fictional

Boeotia (bee-**oh**-sha)
literally "cow land"; flat, grassy region of Greece around Thebes

brazier (**bray**-zher)
coal-filled metal bowl on legs, like an ancient radiator

carruca (kuh-**roo**-kuh)
a four-wheeled traveling carriage, usually mule-drawn and often covered

Castalia (kass-**tale**-yah)
a spring of freshwater on Mount Parnassus, sacred to Apollo

Castor (**kass**-tur)
the mortal one of the mythological twins, the Gemini; Castor is famous for taming horses and Pollux for boxing

caupona (kow-**pone**-uh)
an inn, tavern, or retail shop, usually one that sold alcohol

Cenchrea (ken-**cree**-uh)
(or Cenchreae) Corinth's eastern port; one end of the *diolkos* was here

ceramic (sir-**am**-ik)
clay that has been fired in a kiln, very hard and smooth

Ceramicus (kare-ah-mee-**kuss**)
district of Athens near the Dipylon Gates where potters had their workshops

185

Cithaeron (kith-**eye**-ron)
>   mountain near Thebes where the infant Oedipus was exposed by his parents

Clytemnestra (klite-em-**ness**-tra)
>   wife of Agamemnon, she murdered him the night he returned from Troy

Cnidos (k'**nee**-doss)
>   famous town with a double harbor on a promontory in Asia Minor (modern Turkey)

codex (**koh**-dex)
>   the ancient version of a book, usually made with papyrus or parchment pages

Colonia Corinthiensis (kol-**lone**-ee-uh kore-inth-ee-**en**-siss)
>   Colonia Laus Julia Corinthiensis was the official name given to Corinth when it was reestablished as a Roman colony in 44 B.C. by Julius Caesar

colonnade (kol-a-**nade**)
>   a covered walkway lined with columns

Corinth (**kore**-inth)
>   prosperous and busy Greek port situated on an isthmus between the Ionian and Aegean seas; destroyed in 146 B.C. by Mummium, it was reestablished as a Roman colony and capital of the Roman province of Achaea (Greece) in 44 B.C.

Craneum (kra-**nay**-um)
>   name of a cypress grove that grew in front of the city gates of Corinth

Croesus (**kree**-suss)
>   king of Lydia in the sixth century B.C.; attacked the Persians and was defeated

Cromyon (**krow**-me-on)
>   village near Corinth, terrorized by a man-eating sow until Theseus killed it

Cynic (**sin**-ick)

someone who followed the philosophy of Diogenes, who scorned pleasure and physical comfort and lived in a clay pot like a dog ("cynic" is Greek for "doglike")

Delphi (**dell**-fee)

stunning site on rugged cliffs overlooking the Gulf of Corinth; it was Apollo's main sanctuary and home of the famous Delphic oracle, the Pythia

Delphina (dell-**fee**-nah)

Latin for "female dolphin," the name of Lupus's ship

denarius (den-**are**-ee-us)

small silver coin worth four sesterces

diolkos (dee-**ol**-koss)

paved way with ruts to guide the wheels of carts carrying unloaded ships across the isthmus of Corinth at its narrowest point of about four miles

Dionysus (dye-oh-**nie**-suss)

Greek god of vineyards and wine; he comforted Ariadne on Naxos

Dipylon (**dip**-ill-on)

fortified gate in the city wall of Athens

domina (**dom**-in-ah)

Latin for "mistress" or "madam"; a polite form of address for a woman

Eleusis (ell-**yoo**-siss)

city on the coast near Athens, famous for the mysterious rites celebrated there

Epicurean (ep-ee-cure-**ee**-un)

follower of Epicurus, who esteemed calmness of mind and devotion to pleasure

Erechtheion (air-ek-**thee**-on)

temple on the Acropolis with marble sculptures of women

(called "caryatids") instead of columns; it was dedicated to Athena and Poseidon

Eumenides (you-**men**-id-eez)

Greek for "Kindly Ones," a euphemistic name for the Furies and title of the final play in Aeschylus's trilogy about Orestes

Flavia (**flay**-vee-a)

a Roman girl's name that means "fair-haired"; Flavius is the masculine form

freedman (**freed**-man)

a slave who has been granted freedom; his ex-master becomes his patron

frigidarium (fridge-id-**ah**-ree-um)

the cold plunge in a Roman baths

Furies (**fyoo**-reez)

terrible monsters who looked like women but had snaky hair like Medusa, they pursued people guilty of terrible crimes, especially murder of a relative

Hades (**hay**-deez)

the Underworld, where the spirits of the dead were believed to go

Helicon (**hell**-ik-on)

mountain in Boeotia near Delphi, sacred to Apollo and the Muses

Hephaestus (hef-**eye**-stuss)

Greek name for Vulcan, the god of blacksmiths and metalworking

Hercules (**her**-kyoo-leez)

mythological hero who completed twelve tasks and had many other adventures

hexameter (hex-**am**-it-ur)

type of poetry where each line has a certain number of long and short syllables

hospitium (hoss-**pit**-ee-um)
>   Latin for "hotel" or "guesthouse"; often very luxurious, with
>   baths and dining rooms

hydria (**hid**-ree-uh)
>   special jar for bringing water from the fountain

Hymettus (hi-**met**-uss)
>   mountain near Athens, famed for its honey and for its marble

Hypnos (**hip**-noss)
>   Greek god of sleep, often portrayed as a winged youth who
>   touches the foreheads of the tired with a branch

Iphigenia (if-idge-en-**eye**-uh)
>   daughter of Agamemnon and Clytemnestra, her father sacri-
>   ficed her in order to bring fair winds that would carry the
>   Greek fleet to Troy

Isthmia (**isth**-mee-uh)
>   site near Corinth where athletic games were held in honor of
>   Poseidon

isthmus (**isth**-muss)
>   narrow piece of land connecting two larger pieces of land

Jove
>   another name for Jupiter, king of the gods

Juno (**jew**-no)
>   queen of the gods and wife of the god Jupiter; her Greek
>   equivalent is Hera

Jupiter (**jew**-pit-er)
>   king of the Roman gods and husband of Juno; his Greek
>   equivalent is Zeus

lararium (lar-**ar**-ee-um)
>   household shrine, often a chest with a miniature temple on
>   top, sometimes a niche

lares (**la**-raise)
>   minor deities who protected specific areas, most usually the
>   household

Lechaeum (**lek**-eye-um)
>   western port of Corinth; one end of the *diolkos* was here

Lydia (**lid**-ee-uh)
>   kingdom in Asia Minor (modern Turkey) ruled by Croesus in the sixth century B.C.

Megara (**meg**-are-uh)
>   town between Corinth and Eleusis with two fortified hills

Minerva (min-**erv**-uh)
>   Roman name for Athena, goddess of wisdom and war

Minotaur (**my**-no-tore)
>   mythical monster with a man's body and a bull's head; killed by Theseus

modus operandi (**mo**-duss op-er-**an**-dee)
>   Latin for "way of operating" or "method of doing something"

mulsum (**mull**-some)
>   wine sweetened with honey, often drunk before meals

nereid (**nair**-ee-id)
>   sea nymph; daughter of Nereus, a sea god

Nero (**near**-oh)
>   emperor who ruled Rome from A.D. 54 to A.D. 68

Oedipus (**ed**-ip-uss)
>   king of Thebes who unwittingly killed his father and married his mother

omphalos (ome-fall-**oss**)
>   Greek for "navel"; stone altar at Delphi which represented the center of the world

Orestes (or-**ess**-teez)
>   son of Agamemnon and Clytemnestra, he was commanded by Apollo to avenge his father's murder by killing his mother and was then pursued by the Furies

Orpheus (**or**-fee-uss)
>   mythological lyre player who charmed men, animals, and rocks with his music

Ostia (**oss**-tee-uh)

    the port of ancient Rome and hometown of Flavia

paean (**pee**-un)

    a chant of triumph or praise, sometimes used by Greeks as a battle cry

palla (**pal**-uh)

    a woman's cloak; could also be wrapped around the waist or worn over the head

papyrus (puh-**pie**-russ)

    the cheapest writing material, made from pounded reeds of the same name

Parnassus (par-**nass**-uss)

    high mountain with twin peaks; on its slopes were Delphi and the Castalian Spring

Parthenon (**parth**-uh-non)

    magnificent and famous temple to Athena on the Acropolis in Athens

pelanos (pell-an-**oss**)

    a sacred pie that had to be presented to the priests of Apollo, along with a goat or lamb, before an audience with the Pythia could be granted

penates (pen-**ah**-teez)

    Latin guardian deities of the household and hearth

Plataea (pluh-**tee**-uh)

    city in Boeotia; famous as the site of a Greek victory over invading Persians

Pnyx (pnicks)

    hill near the Areopagus in Athens where the Athenian assembly met

Pollux (**pol**-lucks)

    one of the mythological twins (he was immortal and Castor mortal); he was a skilled boxer and horseman

Polydeuces (polly-**dyoo**-seez)
  Greek version of the name Pollux, Castor's immortal twin
Poseidon (poh-**side**-un)
  Greek god of the sea, the equivalent of the Roman god
  Neptune
Procrustes (pro-**crust**-eez)
  innkeeper and robber who cut or stretched his guests to fit his
  notorious bed
promanteia (pro-man-**tee**-uh)
  the privilege to see the Pythia before anyone else
Propylea (pro-pie-**lee**-uh)
  monumental entrance to the sanctuary of Athena on the
  Acropolis
Pythagorean (pie-thag-or-**ee**-un)
  person who followed the teachings of the famous mathemati-
  cian and philosopher, Pythagoras
Pythia (pith-ee-uh)
  priestess who uttered the responses of Delphic Apollo
Saronic Gulf
  large bay of the Aegean, bordered by Attica to the north and
  the Isthmus of Corinth to the west
Sciron (**skeer**-on)
  mythological robber on the Isthmus who forced travelers to
  wash his feet before tossing them over the cliff to his man-
  eating turtle on the rocks below
scroll (skrole)
  a papyrus or parchment "book," unrolled from side to side as
  it was read
Seneca (**sen**-eh-kuh)
  Stoic philosopher of Nero's time, who wrote about death and
  destiny

sesterces (sess-**tur**-seez)
> more than one sestertius, a brass coin; four sesterces equal a denarius

Sibyl (**sib**-ill)
> female soothsayer or prophetess; the most famous one lived in a cave near Naples

Sinis (**sigh**-niss)
> town and region in central Greece; famous mythological robber who tied his victims to pine trees and then released them

Sparta (**spar**-ta)
> known for its warlike inhabitants who scorned luxury and comfort in their attempt to train mind and body

stele (**stee**-lee)
> Greek work for a "pillar" or "column," usually a grave marker, often marble, usually painted

stoa (**stow**-uh)
> Greek word for "portico" or "colonnade," i.e., a covered walkway lined with columns

Stoic (**stow**-ick)
> Greek philosophy popular in ancient Rome; among other things, its followers cultivated indifference to physical pleasure or pain

stola (**stole**-uh)
> a dress like a long sleeveless tunic worn by married women

stylus (**stile**-us)
> a metal, wood, or ivory tool for writing on wax tablets

Symi (**sim**-ee)
> small island near Rhodes famous for its sponge divers

temenos (**tem**-en-oss)
> sacred marked-out area, usually in a sanctuary

Theagenes (thee-**ah**-gun-eez)
> king of Megara who lived in the seventh century B.C.

Thebes (theebz)
> Greek town in a flat plain between Athens and Delphi; birthplace of Oedipus

Theseus (**thee**-syoos)
> mythological hero, son of Aegeus; set out for Athens aged fifteen to claim his birthright; met many monsters and villains along the way

triclinium (trick-**lin**-ee-um)
> ancient Roman dining area, usually with three couches to recline on

tunic (**tew**-nic)
> a piece of clothing like a big T-shirt; children often wore a long-sleeved one

vespasian (vess-**pay**-zhun)
> Latin slang for "chamber pot," after the emperor who levied a tax on urine

vigiles (**vidge**-il-lays)
> watchmen who guarded Roman towns and provinces against fire and crime

vir (veer)
> Latin for "man"

votive (**vo**-tiv)
> an object offered to mark a vow, prayer, or thanksgiving to some god

vow
> a pledge to a god or goddess which usually took the form "If you do something for me, I will do something for you;" often the latter was the setting up of an altar

wax tablet
> a wax-covered rectangular leaf of wood used for making notes; often two or more are hinged together with twine to make a "book"

Xerxes (**zurk**-sees)

    king of Persia in the early fifth century B.C.; he invaded Greece and was defeated

Zeus (**zyooss**)

    king and greatest of the Greek gods; his Roman equivalent is Jupiter

THE LAST SCROLL

Romans living in the first century A.D. had mixed feelings about Greece. On the one hand, they looked down on the Greeks, because Rome was the conqueror and Greece the conquered. On the other hand, the Romans still admired Greek culture enormously. Greek was the language all educated Romans had to learn. Many Greeks worked for Romans as tutors, secretaries, artists, and musicians. Rome had adopted the Greek gods and given them different names (except for Apollo), and Romans adored the Greek myths. Two of their favorites were the myths of Theseus and Orestes.

Theseus was the young Athenian whose first quest was to reach his rightful kingdom after clearing the land route to Athens of monsters and brigands. Orestes was the son who had to avenge his father's death by killing his own mother. His terrible tale is told in a trilogy of plays that we call *The Oresteia*, by the great Athenian playwright Aeschylus.

By the first century A.D., when this story takes place, Corinth was arguably the most important city in Greece. Situated on a narrow strip of land known as an isthmus, it was a major port in the Mediterranean. In 146 B.C., Corinth had been destroyed by Rome and its walls torn down. Later, in 44 B.C.—more than a hundred years before this story takes place—it was rebuilt as a

Roman colony and became the capital of the Roman province of Achaea (Greece).

There really were ancient maps and guidebooks in the first century A.D. They told travelers how far cities were from one another and where the best places to stay were.

All the characters who appear in this story are fictional, but almost all the places they visit are real. The only place I have made up is the Cave of the Furies. We know it was near the Areopagus but are still not certain exactly where.